My Sister Is
Driving Me Crazy

My Sister Is Driving Me Crazy

~~~~~~~~~~~~~~~~~~~~~~~~~~~~~~~~~~

Mary E. Ryan

SIMON & SCHUSTER BOOKS FOR YOUNG READERS

Published by Simon & Schuster
New York • London • Toronto • Sydney • Tokyo • Singapore

SIMON & SCHUSTER
BOOKS FOR YOUNG READERS
Simon & Schuster Building, Rockefeller Center
1230 Avenue of the Americas
New York, New York 10020

SIMON & SCHUSTER BOOKS FOR YOUNG READERS
is a trademark of Simon & Schuster.
The text for this book is set in 12 pt. Sabon.

Designed by Paula R. Szafranski

Manufactured in the United States of America.

10 9 8 7 6 5 4 3 2 1

Library of Congress Cataloging-in-Publication Data
Ryan, Mary E.
My sister is driving me crazy / by Mary E. Ryan.   p.   cm.
Summary: Tired of being an identical twin, thirteen-year-old
Mattie seeks her own identity.
[1. Twins—Fiction.   2. Sisters—Fiction.   3. Identity—Fiction.]
I. Title.   PZ7.R955My   1991
[Fic]—dc20   90-41263   CIP   AC
ISBN 0-671-73203-X

For Mary Beth,
with love, comets and asparagus

My Sister Is
Driving Me Crazy

one

~~~~~~

Everything seemed so normal that Sunday. Before the hot tub appeared.

Now it was sitting in the yard next door, and the rain was making the reddish wood slick and shiny. For the fourth time since dinner, I went to the window and took a closer look.

From our bedroom I could see a corner of the porch, part of the hedge, and three windows of the house next door. A few lights were on downstairs, but so far I hadn't seen anything of Lyle or Chloe. Or the boy.

Six hours before, I'd been slumped at the kitchen table, watching Pru and Heather play gin rummy and waiting for the rain to stop so we could ride over and see what was playing at the Uptown Cinema.

"Tomorrow let's start a new club," Pru said. "We haven't thought up a decent one in ages."

Ever since fifth grade, when Heather Yamamoto moved to our block, Pru had been inventing secret clubs. There was the Explorer Club, which involved

1

going to secret overgrown corners of the neighbor-hood and pigging out on marshmallows and candy bars. And the M Club, when we played Monopoly every single day until we never wanted to see another hotel. And the Gourmet Club, which didn't last very long since none of us knew how to cook.

Heather sighed. "I'd like to," she said, "but I've got to go to the opera. It's *La Traviata*, my dad's favorite." Mr. Yamamoto was the owner of Yamamoto's Music Store and a big opera fan. He knew all the arias by heart, and sometimes when we were over at Heather's, we'd hear him bellowing along to his Pavarotti records. He didn't have the greatest voice in the world, but he always sounded like he was having a good time.

Heather didn't have the greatest voice in the world either. In fact, Heather was tone-deaf. Unfortunately, that didn't stop Mr. Yamamoto from making her take violin lessons from the time she could walk. He thought that if she practiced enough, eventually she'd become a musical genius. "It's so embarrassing," Heather would moan. "A lot of great violinists are Japanese, so when people see me, they figure I'll be good too. And then, when I get up to play at recitals, I stink!"

Heather's mother was more interested in her brain. She had decided Heather would study hard and go to Stanford. All Heather really wanted to do was design fashions, but so far she hadn't managed to convince anyone but me.

Meanwhile, Pru was still trying to drum up interest in her new club.

"Maybe it's time we let other people join," Heather suggested. "I mean, let's face it. We're starting to run out of ideas."

"And then, if we got enough members, we could charge dues," I put in. "And then we could save up our money and buy something with it. Like a VCR."

Pru turned and fixed me with a look. "That's a terrible idea," she said. "What's the use of having a secret club if we let everybody join? Besides, we'd have to charge a fortune to save enough for a VCR. But don't worry," she told Heather, "I've got lots of good ideas." Pru shuffled the cards and dealt them out. "Come on, let's play another round."

After a while, I got sick of watching Pru win every hand of rummy. Gazing out at the raindrops rhythmically pelting the lawn, I wished with all my heart that something, anything, would happen.

Sometimes very weird things happen when you make a wish.

Just as Pru yelled "Gin!" there was a loud crash, as if a giant box had fallen out of the sky. The crash was followed by a scream, and then the sound of someone yelling loud, interesting curse words. I raced out to the porch.

An enormous van was parked in the middle of McIntire Street. Behind the van, lying on its side in the rain, was something that looked like a huge old-fashioned wash tub.

"I told you not to roll it, Lyle!" a tall blond woman was screaming at a man standing over the tub. "It's probably cracked in a million places!"

"Calm down, Chloe," the man said. He scratched his thinning hair and stared down at the tub. "I told you it wasn't a good idea to bring that thing with us."

"And I told *you* I wasn't leaving Sausalito without it!" Chloe yelled back.

Pru and Heather skidded to a halt behind me. "I think it's a hot tub," I whispered to Pru. "And it's moving in next door!"

But Pru wasn't looking at the tub. She was staring at a slender male shape shuffling back and forth between the moving van and the little Nissan parked in front of it. Ever since, Pru hadn't taken her eyes off the house next door, except to frown at herself in the mirror and then disappear into the bathroom.

I looked out the window at the tub. It hadn't moved. I waited a moment, but there was no sign of life from the house either. With a sigh, I walked back to the bed and picked up my book.

It was called *Mary, Queen of Scots*, and it was practically a foot thick. Getting through the history section at the public library had been my big plan for the summer. Every summer I got these great ideas, like playing every piece in my *Bach for Beginners* piano book, or memorizing a poem a day from my father's college anthology. But somehow my big plans always petered out.

I forced my eyes down on the page. Twice I'd caught myself checking to see how many chapters were left before the actual beheading. So far, there had been a lot of speeches about the English succession but not much blood.

My father began to bang on the bathroom door. "Prune, are you going to be in there forever?"

"I'll be out in a second, Daddy," Pru yelled back. "And don't call me that terrible name. I told you, my name is Pru. *Prooo!*"

Right after dinner, I'd seen Pru slink into the bathroom carrying a stack of fashion magazines. She was probably in there heaping on the forbidden makeup. Pru was lucky if she got out of the house with even a dab of eye shadow. "Not while you live in this house" was Mom's iron-clad rule.

Mom—or Sally, as she made everyone call her—didn't believe in a lot of things. Makeup, hairspray, artificial food additives, and white sugar were just a few. Most people weren't so strict about that stuff, but Sally had more energy than most people. She was small and wiry, with wavy red hair that she knotted on top of her head in a leather clasp. She wore homespun dresses and Peruvian ponchos and had a long list of causes she wasn't afraid to defend whenever the urge struck.

Unfortunately, the urge usually struck when we were standing in a movie line or shopping for groceries.

"How can you sell poison like this to children?" Sally would yell at the checkout clerk, waving a box of Chocolate Kritters, while everyone in the store stared at us and I hid behind a *National Enquirer*, pretending to read up on Elvis's ghost.

Deep down, I knew she was right. But sometimes I wondered what it would be like to have a mother who wore pretty clothes and bought Pepperidge Farm cookies and knew how to keep a low profile.

Actually, the makeup didn't bother me as much as the cookies. Ever since Sally had started writing a nutrition column for the neighborhood paper, everything delicious had disappeared from our kitchen. It was a good thing Dad did the grocery shopping once in a while. His official position was that beer and baloney weren't going to disappear from his diet just because they weren't nutritionally balanced.

And when it came to makeup, Pru's position was clear too. The minute we left the house, she would whip out a compact and mop at her face until she'd coated every pore.

"It's not like you have a bad complexion," I told her. "You're not going to turn people into stone if you don't have a bunch of pink junk on your face."

It sounded reasonable. But Pru got enraged whenever I pointed out the facts. Further proof, I decided, that for identical twins, Prunehilda and I didn't have much in common.

It wasn't always this way. I could remember a time,

not so long ago, when we dressed exactly alike. Sally would take us to the Cut 'n' Curl Salon on Queen Anne Avenue and have our hair cut in identical layered caps. Every morning Pru would stand in front of the closet and say, "The blue dress today?" or "I think we should wear the red jumper." And I'd shrug, because it didn't matter to me what we wore, and say, "Sure, let's wear the blue today."

On the other hand, I thought, maybe the trouble had started much earlier—thirteen years ago, to be exact—when my father named us after his two remaining relatives, Great-aunt Prudence and her sister, Matilda.

Why couldn't he have had remaining relatives with normal names, I used to think, before I realized that Matilda Josephine Darwin was the perfect name for a major American artist. I could just see it printed in a museum guide. *The Matilda Darwin Retrospective: Now on at the Frye Gallery.*

In the meantime we had ended up Prune and Mattie.

At least I had ended up Mattie. Last year, Prune suddenly announced that from now on she would be called Pru, thank you very much. That was the day I privately began calling her Prunehilda. And picking out my own clothes. And mostly, trying to stay out of her way.

It's funny how people look at twins and figure they're best friends. Hah, I thought, as the door flew open and Pru walked in. These days, as far as Prunehilda was concerned, everything I did was wrong. My clothes were wrong and my jokes were wrong. Even the way I made my bed was wrong.

For the millionth time I wished I could have my own room. I already had one picked out—the spare bedroom my father used for a study.

"You already have an office on campus," I'd point out. "Why can't I have a study too? I could use it for my art work. And maybe I could move my bed in there. You know, in case I wanted to take a nap or something."

It seemed like a good approach. But it didn't work. "The day you sell a painting, you can have my study," Dad had said. "Until then, I need it to work on my articles." So far, I hadn't sold any paintings. But that was only because I hadn't had a one-woman show yet.

Someday it would happen, I was sure. I just hoped I would still be living at home when it did.

I peered at Pru. She was moving in a stiff, sneaky way that meant she'd been up to something. I watched her slip over to the window and peek out. "Seen anything yet?" she asked casually. "Of the new people?"

"Nope," I said. I closed my book. "I thought that was pretty interesting though, the way they got the hot tub out of the street."

Pru sighed. "So they called some movers and had them carry it out to the backyard. Big deal. I could have thought of that."

"I wonder what they'll use it for."

"What do you mean, what they'll use it for?" Pru

stared at me. "You mean, will they wash their socks in it? Or bob for apples on Halloween? What do you think you do with a hot tub? You sit in it and drink champagne and stuff! Don't you know anything?"

Incompatibility, I thought. Maybe I could divorce my twin on the ground of irreconcilable differences. "It's like this, Your Honor," I'd tell the judge. "We don't share the same interests anymore. We're going in opposite directions. I just don't think it's going to work out."

My eyes suddenly focused. "Pru? What did you do to your *eyebrows*?"

Pru wet a fingertip and drew it lightly over one eyebrow. "I plucked them," she said. "And you should start doing that too."

I gazed at her blotchy skin. "Didn't it hurt?" I asked.

"A little," Pru said. "It wasn't as bad as I thought it would be." She smiled self-consciously.

"A little?" I grabbed one of her fashion magazines and waved it in Pru's face. "They probably had to put this model under anesthesia to get her eyebrows like that! Anyway, what was wrong with your old ones? I thought they looked fine."

"They looked awful, Mattie! I know you don't care about that stuff, but I do. And that new guy next door is not going to see me wearing these huge Neanderthal eyebrows. Not if I have to have them surgically removed!"

I shrugged. "Okay, I think they're great. Hey, with

eyebrows like that, you're probably all lined up for a glass of champagne in the hot tub."

Pru clamped her lips into a thin, angry line. "Just because you've got a grudge against the whole world, Mattie Darwin," she said, "just because you like to sit here, scribbling in your sketchbooks and writing your depressing poetry—which, by the way, I wish you wouldn't leave all over our room—that doesn't mean you can't try to act normal for a change!"

"Oh, you mean I'm not normal because I don't look like a stove exploded in my face and burned off all my—"

For a moment I thought Pru was going to haul off and punch me. Instead, she grabbed her sweater and stomped out of the room.

I sighed. She was probably going over to Heather's so that Heather could tell her how great her new eyebrows looked. That was the aggravating thing about Heather—she rarely took sides.

On the other hand, it wasn't easy being the best friend of twins. All things considered, Heather did a pretty good job., She probably had a great career in diplomacy ahead of her. That is, if she didn't end up becoming the world's worst concert violinist.

After a moment, I picked up my own sweater and headed downstairs. I could have killed Pru for reading my poetry. And for calling it depressing. Of course it was depressing. People didn't write poetry when life was a piece of cake. For a moment I wished I had a big box where I could lock up my poetry and my drawings and everything about myself I didn't want Pru to find.

Then I realized that was pointless. Pru would figure out a way to pick the lock.

My mother was in the living room, watching a TV show about whales. "Did Pru just leave?" I asked her.

Sally stirred. "I think she went over to Heather's," she said, not taking her eyes off a baby whale being born.

"Does that mean she's finally out of the bathroom?" my father called.

"See you later," I said, and stepped outside.

The rain had stopped and the sky was still light. I stood on the porch for a moment, gazing out at the pale blue evening. Then I moved quickly down the street until I came to a break in the trees where I could see the lights of the city below.

At the foot of the hill was the Seattle Center where the 1962 World's Fair had been held. A lot of buildings from the fair were still there, including the tall arches of the Science Center and the pointed spire of the Space Needle. In the twilight it looked like an elegant spaceship about to take off.

I took a deep breath of rain-washed air. This was the year, I thought, staring up at the sky. The year I'd make my mark. Not as one of the identical Darwins—Darwin Une and Darwin Deux, our confused French teacher used to call us—but as Matilda Josephine

Darwin, a deeply vivacious human being and artiste extraordinaire. A person with a lot to offer the world, if only the world were ready to appreciate her.

Gazing down at the Space Needle, I tried to imagine my destiny. Deep down, I knew it was impossible to see into the future. Things had to work out the way they were supposed to. But all the same, you couldn't just drift along, putting up with the boredom and the monotony. You had to take steps. You had to give destiny a push in the right direction.

Like Pru, I thought grudgingly. Even though her eyebrows looked weird now, at least they were her own. At least she had taken a step.

I stared down the hill at the Space Needle. If this was really the year, maybe it was time I took some steps of my own. I wasn't sure what those would be. But when the time came, Mattie Darwin would be ready.

On the way home, I thought some more about destiny. It was so mysterious the way things fell into place. Like my parents meeting at a student protest rally, totally by accident, and ending up getting married. Or the way our cat, Winston, had shown up on our doorstep, washing his paws and calmly waiting for someone to feed him.

Stuff like that *had* to be destiny, I thought. The only problem was, you couldn't prepare for it. You just had to wait and watch and be ready.

I started up the front steps. Halfway up, I stopped. A

bright light was shining through the hedge. I peered closer. It was coming from the house next door.

I looked around, in case Prunehilda was watching. Then, as quietly as I could, I stole around the side of the house. Crouching down, I peeked through the hedge, straight into an open window.

Ten feet away, a boy sat at a long table unpacking a box. A shiver went through me. He was the most wonderful boy I'd ever seen. He had a square face with smooth features and curly dark-brown hair. And long eyelashes, I was sure. He sat there lifting things out of the box—a catcher's mitt, a volleyball, a tennis racquet—and placing them on the table.

Then he stopped. He seemed to be thinking about something, because he sat still, fingering the webbing on the tennis racquet and looking down at the table.

Destiny, I thought, and shivered again. Tonight, of all nights, I had looked up at the stars and made a vow to the universe. And at the very same moment, these fascinating people were unpacking right next door. It was almost too good to be true.

I suddenly wanted to burst through the hedge and present myself to the boy. I wondered how old he was. Fourteen? Fifteen? It didn't matter. Because here he was, looking like he'd just stepped off a TV show, and sitting a mere ten feet away.

A second later, I was glad I hadn't burst through the hedge after all. Chloe, the blond lady who'd been screaming about the hot tub, walked into the room.

She began saying something, and I strained to hear what it was. Something about all the boxes upstairs, whether he'd seen where the movers had put the kitchen stuff. The boy shook his head, still looking down at his tennis racquet. His mother started to leave.

Then she stopped. "Oh, Cam," she said, practically right into my hedge. "I hope we've done the right thing, coming here."

Cam, I thought. Cameron? Nobody had a name like that, except on the soaps. Cam. I couldn't believe it.

The boy glanced over his shoulder and I could see the corner of his grin. "It'll be okay, Mom," he said in a cute, slightly cracking voice. "You'll see." Then he paused, and his handsome face clouded slightly. "I sure hope I can find a decent court here."

Suddenly he scooped all the sports junk back into the box. Hoisting it onto his shoulder, he followed the blond lady out of the room.

I crouched perfectly still. Tennis. It was a subject I'd never considered before. I wondered if it would be very hard to learn.

I got to my feet. I was about to tiptoe away when I heard a rustling sound. It was the sound a large animal might make if it were stuck in the bushes. And it was only a few feet away.

I froze. Even though Queen Anne is near downtown Seattle, it still has quite a few woods. Sometimes raccoons or bigger animals showed up to root through people's garbage. I didn't want to think about those bigger animals.

Pulling my sweater around me, I peered at the rustling bushes. Whatever was in there began to thrash around. As the branches shuddered and swayed, I turned to run.

Then the bushes gave another twitch, and a second later, Pru struggled out of the hedge, wet leaves spilling off her clothes and hair.

"What are you doing here?" I whispered. "You practically gave me a heart attack!"

Pru looked startled. "I . . . was looking for something." She paused to pick a leaf off her shorts. "I guess my sweater got caught on a branch."

"While you were spying on the new neighbors, you mean."

"I was not!" Pru snapped. She glared at me suspiciously. "Anyway, what were *you* doing out here? Trimming the hedge?"

"Well," I said, "I hope you found whatever it was." Then I hurried off before Cam heard our voices and came out to investigate.

When I reached the back stairs, I paused and glanced at the yard next door. The empty wooden tub stood glistening in the twilight. For a moment, I tried to imagine what it would be like when it was hooked up and bubbling with steaming water. And how it would feel to sit out in the night air, holding a frosty glass of champagne and smiling at a boy named Cam.

two

~~~~~~

The next morning, Sally looked around the breakfast table with a nervous smile. "John? Girls? I have an announcement."

Pru and I exchanged glances. My glance said, "Oh, no. What's it going to be this time?" Pru's glance said, "I don't know. It could be anything. But it better not involve us."

Dad cleared his throat. "Is this going to threaten our food supply?" he asked. He began to look nervous. "We're not having more children, are we?"

I looked at my mom. Her hair was tied in a thick red braid down her back, and her face was pink with excitement. "Of course not, John," she said. "No, this is something entirely different. I've given it a lot of thought," she said, "and I've come to a decision. I, Sally Bradshaw Darwin, am going to open a restaurant. A health-food restaurant. A gourmet 100-percent-natural food restaurant." She looked around the table expectantly. "I hope I'll have the whole-hearted support of my family."

Dad stroked his beard. "Sally, dear, restaurants are pretty risky. Most of them fail the first year. You really should research the market before you—"

"But I have," Sally said firmly. "It's going to be a very small restaurant, which cuts the risk considerably. I've drawn up a business plan, and I've been to the bank. It's all set up, right down to the operating license. Opening next month at the corner of Third and Bell— The Golden Groat, your headquarters for naturally delicious cuisine."

She looked around the table again. "Do you like the name? I picked it out myself. It just seemed to roll off the tongue."

Silence loomed over the breakfast table. I didn't know what a groat was, but I was pretty sure it wouldn't roll off the tongue. Or onto very many, for that matter. I took a bite of my kelp-and-wheatgrass muffin, featured in Sally's latest column. It was dark green, with bits of seaweed poking out of it. It tasted about the way it looked.

"Mom," I said, when I could speak again, "I hate to ask. But who's going to go to a restaurant to eat stuff like seaweed and groats?"

"Not seaweed, Mattie. *Kelp*. There's a big nutritional difference. And lots of health-minded people will come. Vegetarians. Macrobiotics . . ."

"Condemned prisoners," Pru muttered. But Sally didn't seem to notice. Humming under her breath, she got up and began to clear the table.

I glanced at Pru. Then we both turned and glared at our father.

He squirmed. "Well, Sal," he began, "this is certainly a surprise."

Dad always seemed a little amazed by Sally. He was almost fifteen years older than she was. He had been head of the history department when Sally was in college studying guerilla theater. According to family legend, they had gotten into a big fight during a protest rally and wound up going out for coffee afterward. Ever since, Dad claimed, life had been one surprise after another.

"Yes, I suppose this *is* unexpected," Sally said. "But I didn't want to spring it on you until I'd finished signing the papers and figuring out the menu. And my first idea, girls, involves you."

She picked up her mug of peppermint tea and took a sip. "I thought," she said, "we could throw a big party for the neighborhood. You kids could invite all your friends, and we could have some of the parents over. You know, a sort of grassroots get-together."

"With real grass for refreshments," I said helpfully.

She ignored my suggestion. "I've been reading up on this stuff, and it's a great way to spread the word. Grab the kids, and their parents' stomachs will follow!"

"But, Mom—" Pru said.

"And at the same time, I thought it would be a nice way to get to know the people next door."

A different mood settled over the table. "Yes," Dad remarked, "I noticed all the vans with California plates. Kind of wondered when the old Webster place would finally sell."

Sally nodded thoughtfully. "California . . . I wonder if they know of any good seafood recipes. Well, I'll ask them about it tonight."

"Tonight?" Pru yelped.

"Doesn't that seem a little soon?" I asked.

"Not when the grand opening is only a few weeks away," Sally replied. "In the meantime, let's think of this as an old-fashioned end-of-summer bash. A way for everyone to get to know each other."

She turned to Pru and me. "Why don't you two run next door and ask the new family if they can stop by? And I'll get going on the food."

"Not macrobiotic food, Mom," I said. "It's a party, remember?" But Sally had already danced off to make her lists.

My dad took a bite of his kelp muffin. "Girls," he announced when he'd finished chewing, "I'm afraid she's really got us this time."

"Well, can't you tell her not to?" Pru said. "You know how carried away Mom gets!"

Dad shrugged. "It would be like trying to stop a force of nature," he said. "Believe me, Prune, I've tried."

He stood up. "Ever seen pictures of a hurricane hitting a small town? Well, just think of us as that town." He grinned. "Whoosh."

Whistling, he stepped out the back door and headed off for campus.

I watched him go. I envied my father. He had his nice quiet office at the university, where he could read his books about World War II sea battles and grade his papers and pretend that Hurricane Sally didn't exist.

"Maybe we can still talk her out of it," I told Pru. She was busy admiring her new eyebrows in the shiny side of the toaster.

Pru looked up. "Actually," she said, "maybe it's not such a bad idea. Like Mom said—parties are a great way to get to know people."

Sure, I thought. People with a hot tub.

Winston strolled into the kitchen looking for something to eat. I fed him a crumb of kelp. He looked disappointed and began to bat it around the floor. "Well, okay," I said. "If that's how you feel, let's call Heather and figure out who to invite."

"Fine." Pru stood up. "You call Heather, and I'll run next door and tell the new neighbors about the party."

"Hey, wait a minute! Mom said we were *both* supposed to invite them."

Pru shrugged. "Just trying to save you the trouble."

"It's no trouble," I said. "I'll be ready in a flash."

Up in our room, I stood in front of the mirror and

tried to picture what Cam would see when we showed up on his porch.

Not much, I decided. I hadn't washed my hair, and it hung to my shoulders like reddish-brown straw. My face looked okay—a little too round, but tan and healthy from the sun. But when I peered closer, I saw a pink blotch on my chin. The longer I peered, the bigger it seemed to get.

Great, I thought. One look at that and Cam wouldn't be able to eat for a week. That is, if he survived Sally's naturally delicious cuisine.

Emergency situations called for emergency measures. Sacrificing all my principles, I reached for Pru's makeup kit. Quickly I began to dab some tawny beige cover-up on my blotchy chin.

Then I noticed Pru's brand-new coral-pink lipstick. First impressions count, I told myself. After all, Cam was used to California girls drenched in makeup. A little lipstick couldn't hurt.

When I was done, I looked at myself. A tawny beige creature with flamingo-pink lips stared back. Pru began yelling at me to hurry up, but all I could do was stare at my face in horror.

Finally I grabbed a Kleenex and began to scrub. Two minutes later, my face looked as hideously tawny as ever.

Oh well, I thought. At least no one would notice the zit on my chin. "Ready!" I called, and dashed downstairs.

Pru was waiting at the back door. I was glad to see that her eyebrows looked even weirder than they had last night. "Let's go," I said.

"Shouldn't we change first?"

"Change?" I looked down at my clothes: white jeans and a University of Washington T-shirt. "Why?" I said. "What do you think we should wear? Prom gowns?"

Pru paused. "I just thought it might be cute if we wore the same thing. You know, twin stuff."

"Twin stuff?" I stared at her. "Don't you think we're getting a little old for that routine?"

"It was just an idea." Her face stiffened resentfully. "I thought the new neighbors might think it was kind of cute and unusual to have twins next door. But if you don't want to, that's fine with me."

"Pru," I sighed. "Once they see us, I think they'll get the message."

Pru glared at me. Then she turned and marched down the back steps.

She stopped when we reached the hedge. "On second thought," she said, "why don't you ask them, Mattie? I mean, you're right. One of us should start calling people from school."

"You're the one who thought it would be cute and unusual to pull the old twin act," I said. "I think we should both ask him—I mean, them."

"Okay," Pru said. "But you knock."

"Why me?" I remembered in Camp Fire Girls when we had to sell candy door-to-door. My heart would jam in my throat and my hands would sweat. By the time the people opened their doors, I would feel like tossing the candy at their feet and running away.

Well, we weren't selling candy this time. "Come on," I told Pru. "We'll tell them about Mom's party and then leave."

"Okay. But you go first."

"What's the matter? Don't you want to do the talking?"

Pru gave me a thin smile. "You do it," she said. "You're the one who's wearing all the makeup. Maybe they'll think you're the Avon lady."

I felt my face turning pinker than Pru's lipstick. But it was too late—she was already shoving me toward the stairs. I took a deep breath. Then I climbed the front steps of the old Webster place and pressed the bell.

As the doorbell echoed through the house, I seriously thought about diving into the nearest hedge.

Then I heard footsteps, and the door opened. It was the blond woman I'd seen the night before. Chloe.

"Yes?" She looked at me and then at Pru, who was huddled behind my shoulder.

I gulped. "Er, we live next door. And our mom is opening a restaurant . . ."

Pru popped her head out. "And she's throwing this big party tonight to promote it. And she wanted to know if you—"

"And your family," I added firmly.

"—could come," Pru finished.

The woman didn't say anything. Then a delighted smile crossed her face. "You're twins, aren't you! Lyle, look, we have twins next door!"

A moment later, a man in a maroon jogging suit appeared at the door. "How do you do," he said. "I'm Lyle Davis, and this is my wife, Chloe. And you're our new neighbors!"

"Yes," I said hastily. "I'm Matilda Darwin, and this is my sister, Prudence."

"Pru," Pru put in.

"Oh, I'm so sorry, I forgot to introduce myself," Chloe exclaimed. "But I just adore twins! The ancient civilizations thought they were good luck, you know. Except for a few barbarians who thought they were *bad* luck and threw them off cliffs. But they weren't very enlightened," she hastened to assure us.

"Would you girls like to come in for a moment?" Lyle interrupted. "We just moved in, so please excuse the mess."

When we stepped inside, I didn't see any mess. The living room was full of stark white furniture. Modern lighting hung from the ceiling. At one end of the room I noticed an elaborate computer station.

"We're invited to a party next door. Isn't that charming? So friendly!" Chloe exclaimed. She turned to Pru and me. "Would you guys like a lime-and-kiwi sparkler? I just discovered them at the store and now I'm addicted."

"Sure," I said, as Chloe sped off to the kitchen.

Lyle sat down at the computer table. "Forgive my wife," he said, smiling. "I guess you could say Chloe's a people kind of person. But sometimes she gets carried away."

"That's okay," I said. "Our mom's like that too. Anyway," I went on, "we just wanted to welcome you to the neighborhood." Where, I wondered, was Cam? "So, if you can come—"

"—We'd love to have you," Pru finished.

"Great," Lyle said. He crossed one ankle over his knee. "You know, this is just what we were hoping to find when we moved up here. Neighborliness. I'm a software designer, and I noticed the Northwest was developing a real cutting edge in the field. So we decided to move the center of operations up here."

Lyle's voice took on a smooth professional flow as he began to describe the many uses of software and the different programs he was working on. I wondered if Lyle thought Pru and I were his clients.

All of a sudden he seemed to notice we were just thirteen-year-old girls, because his voice returned to normal. "Anyhow, we figured Seattle would be a warm, community-oriented place to settle. Didn't we, darling?"

Chloe came bustling into the room. She handed each of us a tall glass. "What's that, dear?"

"Seattle. How it seemed like a people kind of place."

"Oh, yes!" She settled cozily on the white sofa. "Did Lyle tell you he designs software?"

We nodded.

"Well, I just know he's going to do fabulously up here. We tried Silicon Valley, but . . ." Chloe made a face. "Too sterile, too high-tech. Actually, I'm hoping to drum up a little interest in my sideline too. It's—"

But before we could hear about Chloe's sideline, the door to the kitchen flew open. "Mom? Are there any more cinnamon . . .?"

It was the boy. Cameron.

He was even better up close. And I was right about the eyelashes. They were long and curly, framing eyes the color of a robin's egg and matching his dark hair, which just touched the collar of his blue-and-white rugby shirt.

"Cam, meet Prudence and Matilda," Lyle said. "Our next-door neighbors. Girls, our son, Cam."

"How do you do," Pru said passionately.

"Hi," I murmured, arranging my lips in a demure smile. I hoped he liked coral-pink lipstick.

"Nice to meet you," the boy said in a mechanical voice. He turned to his mother. "Listen, are there any of those cinnamon rolls left? Or did Zee scarf them all?"

She frowned. "There should be some. Check the refrig."

"Okay," he said. With a nod, he turned on his Adidas and jogged back to the kitchen.

I took a long sip of kiwi juice. Cam hadn't seemed to notice my coral-pink lipstick. Or the fact that we were cute, unusual twins. He hadn't seemed to notice anything about us at all.

Maybe Pru was right, I thought gloomily. The old twin act might have been the way to go.

Then I remembered my vow. If this was the year I was going to make my mark, I had to learn how to be patient. Besides, I thought, Cam was probably hungry. You couldn't expect a person to be rational and observant when he was starving to death. Especially when there were cinnamon rolls involved.

I set my glass on the coffee table. "I'm afraid we have to be going," I said, giving Pru a sharp nudge. "We've still got a lot to do before the party."

"Shall we come by about eight?" Chloe asked.

"Eight is fine," Pru said. She seemed unwilling to leave, but I got firmly to my feet.

"Anything we can bring?" Lyle asked. He got up too, and walked us out to the front hall.

"Just yourselves," Pru said. "All of you, I mean. That is—"

"It's just a bunch of families getting together," I explained. "The more, the merrier."

"That's our style," Lyle said. "Listen, thanks for coming by. We hope our two families will be seeing a lot of each other. Don't we, Chloe?"

Chloe followed us out to the porch. "Definitely," she said. "And I can't wait to meet your mom. I'm a real gourmet myself. I'll bet we have a lot in common."

"Thank you for the drink," I said. Then I herded Pru

down the front steps while Lyle and Chloe stood at the door waving.

As soon as we got around the corner, I started to laugh.

"What's so funny?" Pru demanded. "And how come you dragged us out of there? We were just getting to know them!"

Her expression made me laugh even harder. "I'm sorry, Pru," I said. "There was just something about them. About Lyle and Chloe. The sparkling kiwi juice, and the software, and the maroon jogging suit, and the—the . . ."

Pru stood gazing at me furiously. "You know what your problem is, Mattie?" she said finally. "You just aren't a people kind of person!"

And with that, my sister swept up the back stairs to get things ready for the party.

three

~~~~~~~~~~~~~~~~~~~~~~~~~~~~~~~~~~~~~

By mid-afternoon, the kitchen was full of food.

At least I thought it was food. Then I looked closer. One plate was covered with white things rolled up in dessicated leaves. I poked one gingerly, but it didn't move.

My mother laughed. "Don't look so worried, Mattie. It's sushi, a great Japanese delicacy."

"What's sushi?" I asked.

"If I tell you, you won't want to try it. Sushi," she explained, "is raw fish wrapped in seaweed. It's really quite delicious," she added, as I made a gagging sound.

She pointed at some yellow lumps. "And these are cheese puffs made with real goat's cheese. I found the authentic Tibetan recipe, can you believe it?"

She began arranging a wreath of salt-free pickles around the cheese puffs. "This is so much fun! I can't imagine why we've never thrown a party before."

"We did," Pru said. "When we were ten. You made us give a Halloween party and nobody showed up."

"Well, I promise that won't happen tonight," Sally said. "I've called just about everyone I know, and your dad's invited a few people from the college." Then she frowned. "Did you remember to ask the people next door?"

"Yes," Pru said. "They said they'd be by around eight."

"And Heather called some of the kids from school." I picked up a bowl and sniffed it. "What's this white junk? Dip or something?"

"Whipped tofu, darling. For the crudités."

"The what?"

"Raw vegetables," Pru said. "Don't you know anything?"

I ignored her. "Mom," I said. "You promised to go easy on the health food."

"I know." Sally looked sheepish. "But I came across this recipe while I was researching my column, and it sounded absolutely delicious."

I sampled the tofu. "Guess again," I said.

"Hush, Mattie. Now, why don't you guys get the living room set up? You can use Dad's stereo from the study."

I grabbed a pickle and followed Pru to my father's office, where we unhooked his big stereo and hauled it out to the living room. Then I went to get our tapes. When I came back, Pru was sitting on the rug, looking through my parents' records.

"These are unbelievable," she said. "How could they hang on to such dumb-sounding albums?"

"Let me see." I peered over her shoulder. "Strawberry Alarm Clock. Moby Grape. Sonny and Cher."

"Sonny and Cher?" She grabbed the record. "This must be worth a fortune!"

Actually, I liked my parents' music, even the corny psychedelic stuff. But it made me feel weird to picture my mother and father wearing bellbottoms and beads, dancing under a flickering strobe light. It made me feel even weirder to realize that when I had kids, they'd think the music I had liked and the clothes I had worn were just as stupid.

"I wonder if the guy next door will come tonight," I said. "Cam Davis."

Pru's head snapped up. "If he doesn't, it'll be your fault."

"Mine? You didn't even have the guts to walk up to his front door!"

"We were hardly there two minutes when you made us leave," Pru said. "Personally, I thought that was rather rude."

"Pru." I tried to keep my voice calm and patient. "He wasn't in the room thirty seconds. Anyway, I thought you laid it on plenty thick about how welcome they were. About how they should bring the *whole* family."

"I wonder if they have any other kids," Pru said. "Lyle and Chloe, I mean."

I didn't answer. A nervous feeling had started in my stomach the minute I'd pictured Cam Davis. It was the same nervous feeling I always got when one of my terrible crushes was about to start.

The last one was two months ago. He was sixteen and worked at the ice-cream stand down by the lake, and his name was Robert. He had blond hair and blue eyes, and my heart just about burned a hole in my chest every time I saw him.

But I was barely in eighth grade, so even if he liked me—and he seemed to, slipping me ice-cream bars and telling me jokes—there was no way I could compete with the high school girls who hung all over the ice-cream stand like idiotic barnacles. So all summer I sat on the beach and watched Robert as he scooped ice cream and flashed his gorgeous smile, but never just for me.

I pictured Cam. He seemed every bit as wonderful as Robert. But this time, I thought, I'd know what to do. This time everything would be different.

If I could only keep Pru out of the picture. When it came to boys, having a twin was definitely no help. The boys we'd met at the lake, for instance, had seemed awfully interested in identical twins, but not very interested in Pru or me. By the time they finished asking their stupid questions ("So how do your parents tell you apart? With name tags or something?") I felt like some kind of weird science-fair project.

Pru was polishing the big china breakfront. "Have

you finished that stuff yet?" she called over her shoulder. "I need you to help me do something."

"In a minute." I was looking down at the carton of tapes. And then I got a fabulous idea.

One by one, I took the cassettes out of their boxes and began to arrange them in the carton in order of danceability. That way, during the party the best tapes would be all ready to play.

Maybe I could get a job doing this at a radio station, I thought, admiring the straight row of cassettes. "Ms. Darwin's coming in to arrange the tapes," the station manager would tell people. And then I'd show up and—

"What are you doing?" Pru stood over me, glaring down at the box of tapes. "You're not supposed to leave them out like that! They'll get dust all over them!"

"I thought it would be easier this way," I said. I grabbed a tape from the box. Somehow my idea didn't seem so brilliant now. "See? We can just pick out a tape and—"

"That's so stupid, I can't believe it." Sighing loudly, Pru walked away and began to push the chairs and tables against the wall.

I looked down at my box of tapes. It wasn't a stupid idea, I told myself. Tonight at the party, when Cam asked me to dance, I would point casually at the box. "Pick a tape," I'd say, "any tape. They're prearranged."

"But of course," he would answer. "Back in California, we always pre-arranged our tapes."

"Come here, Mattie." Pru was dragging a box out from under the coffee table. "You have to help me hide these."

She reached in the box and pulled out a handful of candy bars. I peered over her shoulder. The box was full of junk food. "What do you mean, hide them?"

Pru paused with a cupcake package in one hand and a bag of pretzels in the other. "You saw that awful stuff Mom is making. Nobody in their right mind would actually *eat* that. We can't let people starve." She began stuffing candy bars in strategic corners of the sofa.

"Isn't it kind of weird to make people sit on the refreshments?" I asked.

Pru stuck the bag of pretzels behind one of the stereo speakers. "I'm just hiding it from Mom," she explained patiently. "Just until the party starts. Here," she said, handing me a bag of cheese curls.

"I don't know," I said. "I never heard of hiding food at a party before."

Pru snatched the bag away and shoved it behind Dad's *Encyclopedia of World War II*. "Fine, Mattie," she said. "You can eat raw fish, if you think it's so great. Personally, I would rather be a thoughtful hostess and provide good-tasting snacks for my guests."

Personally, *I* thought this was the craziest idea Pru had come up with yet. She must have been reading one of those articles with names like "How to Throw a

Successful Teen Bash." No one in real life said things like "providing good-tasting snacks for my guests." No one, that is, except Pru.

I watched her stick a package of Twinkies on top of the bookcase. "There!" she exclaimed. "Now, don't forget where we hid all this stuff. We'll need some extra time to make sure it's attractively displayed."

I snapped my fingers. "I know!" I said. "Why don't we order a pizza? We could display it on Dad's turntable. That would be an attractive and different serving concept. Revolving pepperoni!"

Actually, I thought it was a pretty good idea. But Pru just glared at me and then bent down to shove one last Snickers bar into the sofa.

I watched Pru walk over to inspect the box of tapes. We'll just see, I thought, as she paused to hide a bag of marshmallows inside the box. We'll just see who's stupid around here.

"How was the opera?" I asked Heather. It was almost seven o'clock, and we stood in front of the bedroom mirror, trying out different hairstyles.

"Too long, for one thing. I fell asleep during the second act. But the scenery was great." Heather held a fistful of black hair above her head to see how it would look in a vertical style. "Plus she dies in the last act, and it took forever. How are you supposed to believe she's dying when she's running all over the stage, singing her head off? She looked pretty healthy to me."

One thing about Heather, she's very literal-minded.

"So how many kids did you call?" Pru asked. We checked each other's hair. That was one advantage of having a twin—you didn't need a mirror to tell how you'd look in a ponytail.

"Oh, tons. Everyone I could think of."

We went to a progressive junior high called the Puget Sound Academy. "Progressive" meant we had art and drama four times a week and a workshop on current events every Monday. "Junior high" meant the grades included seventh through ninth.

"They all said they'd try to make it," Heather reported.

"I hope everyone notices them," Pru said. She was peering at herself in the mirror.

"Mom's flyers for the Golden Groat?" I said. "How can they help it? She's plastered the whole house with them."

"Not the flyers," Pru said impatiently. "My new eyebrows! Don't you remember? I *plucked* them." Pru studied herself in the mirror. "I think they make a huge difference," she said. "Don't you?"

Nobody said a word.

At seven-thirty people began to arrive for the end-of-summer natural food party. By eight o'clock, they were starting to leave.

I sat on the couch between Heather and Pru. Across the room, a boy named Ron was looking at one of my father's military history books. Everyone else stared politely into space.

Pru's successful teen bash hadn't exactly panned out either. Sally had spent so long arranging her Tibetan cheese puffs and putting up her flyers that we didn't have time to excavate the snacks. So far, no one had noticed them, except for Ron, who looked pretty amazed to find a bag of cheese curls stuffed behind *The Encyclopedia of World War II*.

"I know!" Heather said brightly. "Let's dance. Once people see us, they'll want to, too. It'll break the ice."

Personally, I didn't think a meteor traveling at the speed of light could break the ice at this party. Besides, I didn't want Cam to show up and see me dancing with Heather. She wasn't the worst dancer I'd ever seen. But she made me wonder if a person could be rhythm-deaf and tone-deaf at the same time. As Heather began to hop around the floor, I figured it was a good thing Mr. Yamamoto didn't run a dance academy.

Maybe I could get one of the boys to dance. I glanced at Ron. He was short and chubby and had bright red hair that stuck up like the bristles on a paintbrush. When he saw me looking at him, his face turned the color of his hair.

"I don't like this song," I told Heather. "Let me put on something else." I went to the corner where I'd left the pre-arranged tapes and reached in the box. A second later, Winston shot out like a black rocket and disappeared down the hall.

I stared down at the box. It was filled with mangled marshmallows, and something else. Something that looked like shiny brown spaghetti.

Then I realized it wasn't spaghetti.

"What's wrong? " Sally stood behind me. She was holding a bowl of steamed kelp, even though so far no one had touched the food.

"What's wrong? Winston got in our tapes and ruined them, that's what's wrong!" I didn't mention the marshmallows.

"You can still play your records," Sally said soothingly.

"Not our records, Mom—*your* records. I told you we should have gotten a CD player. This party was bad enough. Now we don't even have music!"

Before she could answer, the doorbell rang. I froze. But it wasn't Cam.

"Bev!" my mother cried. I stifled a groan. Bev Adams was the editor of the *Queen Anne Gazette,* the paper that published Sally's column, and one of Sally's best friends. She had orange hair and drove a silver Corvette and wore shark's tooth earrings. She had a loud, nasal voice that bored through your head like a dentist's drill. A little of Bev Adams could practically wreck a person's day.

Before Bev could fire up the dentist's drill, the doorbell rang again. It was more friends of my parents, Jim and Katie Sawyer, and a few of the Sawyers' friends.

They tumbled into the hall, carrying bags of potato chips and jugs of Washington State wine.

Pru hovered next to me. "I don't think they're coming," she whispered.

"It's still early," I said.

I glanced around the room. Ron had put down the book; he was grabbing Tibetan cheese puffs and stuffing them into his face. Two more boys wandered over and peered hopefully at the Sawyers' potato chips.

Just when I'd decided that things were looking up, I saw my mother waving an album cover in the air. "Remember this?" she called to Bev.

Pru grabbed my arm. "Oh, no. What's she doing?"

I watched Sally walk over to the turntable. "I think," I said, "the sixties are about to live again."

Sure enough, an ancient Beatles song came on the stereo. Soon the living room was full of grownups laughing and leaping and twitching to "Yellow Submarine." It was a frightening sight.

"So what's the deal?"

I looked down. Ron's red hair was poking up next to my shoulder. "Your parents smoke pot or something?" he asked.

"Of course not," I said indignantly. "Do yours?"

By the time the record was over, the house was full of ancient Beatle fans, all of them drinking wine and raving about Sally's steamed kelp. I sighed and grabbed a pretzel out of the nearest stereo speaker. "I wish we could get rid of all these people," I muttered to Heather, as Bev Adams's laughter shook the house.

"I could go home and get my violin," Heather suggested. "That might drive them away."

"Can you play any Beatles songs?"

Heather looked doubtful. " 'Yesterday.' But I haven't practiced it in a while."

"That's okay," I said quickly. "I was just kidding." I handed her a pretzel. "Come on, let's go upstairs. Maybe there's a good movie on TV."

As we started for the stairs, there was a loud knock at the front door. I went over to open it, and the pretzel dissolved in my mouth. There, framed against a spectacular Seattle sunset, stood Lyle and Chloe.

They both wore loose-fitting white clothes. Lyle was carrying a bottle of California wine. A sullen-looking girl dressed in black stood behind them.

"Well!" Lyle exclaimed. "Sounds like quite a bash going on over here."

"Yes," I said. I peered nervously through the open door.

"We're a teensy bit late," Chloe said apologetically. "We had to drop Cam off at the movies. But we got here as soon as we could."

I stared at her. "At the . . . movies?"

"Yes," Chloe said. "*Curse of the Gargoyles* was playing down the street, and it's not out on video yet. He had his heart set on seeing it." She glanced around the room. "Is that your mom? With the beautiful red hair?"

"That's her," I said.

"We're dying to meet her," Chloe said. "But first I'd like to present our daughter, Zee. Well, Zoe, actually." She smiled. "That was Lyle's idea. Chloe and Zoe. Pretty unique, huh?"

I pointed at the refreshment table. "There's Cokes and potato chips back there, if you don't like Tibetan goat cheese."

Zee brushed back her spiky bangs, gave me a long stare, and drifted silently into the house. "She's sixteen and very musical," Chloe confided. "Had her own band back in Sausalito. But she's going through a non-verbal stage at the moment. Now, come on." She took my hand. "Let's go meet your parents."

I led Lyle and Chloe past my father, who was lecturing on the battle of Midway to anyone who would listen, sidestepped Heather and Ron, who were shuffling dismally to the sounds of the Strawberry Alarm Clock, and headed over to where Sally was giving Bev Adams an impromptu interview. "Mom? These are the new neighbors."

Sally looked up. "Oh, *hello*," she said. "So you are the Davises. We've heard so much about you."

"And I can't wait to hear about your restaurant," Chloe exclaimed. "I have a recipe for octopus tempura you'll have to taste to believe."

Then, as I watched, she took something out of her white tunic. "But first, I must tell you about the line of tapes I'm marketing. *The Sounds of Sunset.* Very spiritually soothing. I know you're going to love them."

Pru sidled up. "Well? Did he —?"

"He went," I said, "to see *Curse of the Gargoyles.*"

"He went to some crummy movie?"

"That's right," I said. "But they brought their daughter."

"Is she that zombie girl sitting in our kitchen eating the tofu?"

"Probably," I said.

We were interrupted by the clash of wind chimes, followed by some weird chanting.

"What's that?" Pru asked.

"I think," I said, "we just found out what Chloe's sideline is."

Chloe was sitting next to Sally, describing her books and tapes. "I also handle an excellent line of channeling manuals," she added.

"Chloe's a master channeler," Lyle put in. "Recognized by the New World Spiritualist Foundation. She's contacted quite a few manifestations in the last couple of years."

Sally gulped. "Manifestations?" she said weakly.

"You know. Spirits from another time. They select a human vehicle to pass their wisdom on to us."

"They seem very happy to use me as their channel," Chloe said modestly.

Sally nodded as Zee drifted past carrying the whipped tofu. "The children tell me you have a son about their age," she said. "Have you decided on any schools yet?"

"No," Chloe said. "Can you recommend a good one?"

"Well, the twins go to Puget Sound Academy. It has an excellent reputation. Tons of curricular enrichment."

Chloe glanced at Lyle. "It sounds wonderful," she said. Then she sighed. "Cammy will be in ninth grade this year. I can hardly believe he's out of diapers."

"Oh, I know," Sally agreed. "They grow up before your eyes, don't they?"

Suddenly a puzzled look crossed my mother's face. She reached under the sofa cushion and pulled out a Baby Ruth bar. She sat there frowning at it.

Pru came up and began to pester Chloe with questions about channeling. My mother was staring at the candy bar as if it were a visitor from another galaxy. Somewhere in the distance, Bev Adams began to laugh.

But I didn't care. I didn't even mind when Ron marched up and demanded that someone take "that pukey moaning stuff" off the tape deck. So Cam Davis was a ninth grader. And it looked like he was going to our school.

All of a sudden I couldn't wait for summer to be over.

four

~~~~~~

When the door closed on the last guest, Sally gazed around triumphantly. "There isn't a speck of food left!" She held up an empty bowl. "I knew that tofu spread was a good idea."

"Mom," Pru said, "the only person who touched it was the zombie girl from next door. And she probably thought it was food from her home planet." Pru giggled.

"If that's what tofu does to a person, I'll stick to Big Macs," my father sighed. He picked some paper cups off the bookcase. Then his hand touched the Twinkies and he stared at them for a moment. "Sally darling," he said, unwrapping a Twinkie and biting into it, "will you please check with us before you decide to throw your hat in the ring for mayor?"

"Certainly, John," she said briskly. "But you have to admit everything went very well. Everyone had a good time. And I think I stirred up a lot of grassroots support, especially from our new neighbors."

"Guess what, Mom?" Pru said. "Mrs. Davis invited me over to learn more about channeling. She said I probably had a spiritual affinity, being a twin and all."

She shot me a smug glance. I got up and began to help my father stack the dirty dishes.

"You look tired, sweetie." Sally came over and began to smooth the hair back from my forehead, which is something she always does when she thinks I'm mad at her. "I'm sorry about your tapes. But I'm sure there's no real damage." She paused. "Do you think your friends enjoyed the party?"

What could I say? That no one had said a word after her friends took over? That three of the boys had turned her Golden Groat flyers into paper airplanes? That I wished I'd gone to see *Curse of the Gargoyles* instead?

"Sure," I said. "Great party, Mom."

Later, I lay in bed wondering what the Davises would tell Cam when he came home from the movie. Chloe would probably rave about Sally and her sushi. "And one of the twins has a real interest in channeling, Cammy. I think you'd really like her."

I groaned and rolled over on my stomach. Pru, I decided, was about to discover she wasn't the only twin with a mysterious spiritual gift.

"What a bunch of baloney! You're just trying to horn in on my invitation!"

"Honest, Pru. I swear, right before I fell asleep last night, I had this weird vision. A giant pyramid was hovering right over our house. And then I heard this voice talking in my ear. Something about gargoyles, I think. Or maybe it was hot tubs."

"Mom?" Pru tore down the stairs. "Mattie's making fun of me. Tell her she can't come. Mrs. Davis didn't invite her, she invited meeee!"

"What's all this?" Sally appeared at the foot of the stairs, her reading glasses perched on top of her head.

"Last night, Mrs. Davis—Chloe—said I could come over, and—"

"Pru, I'm in the middle of my column, and I don't appreciate being interrupted." Sally frowned.

"But—"

"I'm sorry, but if your sister wants to visit the neighbors, she has every right to do so. And incidentally, Pru, I'd like to know what a bag of Snickers bars is doing in my typewriter."

There wasn't a sound out of Pru.

"Furthermore, I noticed the amount of makeup you were wearing last night. It's going to wreck your complexion. At least," my mother sighed, "promise me you'll use a good oatmeal scrub when you wash your face. Now, I'm going back in the kitchen," Sally said, "and I'm closing the door, and I don't want to hear another word."

I waited until I heard the door shut. Then I ran downstairs. "Come on," I said. "We'd better head over there before I have any more visions. I might go into convulsions or something."

"Oh, shut up," Pru grumbled. But she followed me down the front steps and across the lawn.

Chloe beamed when she saw us. "I'm so glad you both came," she exclaimed. I shot Pru a meaningful glance. "The vibrations will be much stronger with a double entity present."

She arranged a number of objects on the coffee table. "These will encourage the spirit to manifest itself," she explained, setting a handful of shiny stones next to a glass box. "Crystals have a very potent effect on the metaphysical universe. Great for cramps too. I have a wonderful catalog you can show your mom in case she'd like to order some."

"Thank you," Pru murmured. She stared down at the crystals.

"Now," Chloe continued, "we'll just draw these blinds and bring everything down a few notches. Remember," she said, "these are very ancient beings, and they don't like harsh light or loud noises. So you must be very quiet."

We nodded as Chloe shut the blinds. Then she seated herself on a mat next to the table of crystals.

"Should we close our eyes?" Pru asked.

"That's not necessary," Chloe said. "Don't worry, I don't have any ghosts hidden under the table. It's all very natural. Now just relax, girls, and we'll see if we have a visitor today."

Nervously, we watched Chloe lower her head and begin to breathe deeply. After a moment, her shoulders gave a twitch. Then her head began to jerk violently back and forth. I gripped Pru's hand.

"I am Kronis," Chloe suddenly intoned in a deep, husky voice. "What do you desire of me?"

There wasn't a sound in the room. Then Chloe/Kronis spoke again.

"In the ancient world, I was a powerful Druid. I am ready to teach your world the magic of our ways. But only if your people are willing to learn. When you are ready, I shall come again and enlighten you with the mysteries of our Druid lore."

Chloe's voice faded to a hoarse whisper. Her head dropped to her chest, and she sat perfectly still.

A moment later, her eyes popped open. She looked around expectantly. "Well? Did he come?"

"Who?" Pru asked faintly.

"Oh, there's a couple of them. Peter, from the court of Catherine the Great. Samu, an ancient Phoenician. But my favorite's Kronis, the Druid guy."

"That's the one," Pru said eagerly. "Kronis."

"Don't you remember what happened?" I asked.

Chloe shrugged. "It's up to them," she said. "Sometimes they let you remember, sometimes they don't."

A worried look crossed her face. "He didn't say anything rude, did he? Kronis isn't always in a good mood. Druids are like that, you know. Kind of touchy."

"He was very polite," I assured her. "He talked about some kind of Druid magic that he wanted to teach people."

"Oh, good!" Chloe bounced happily on her mat. "You see? Nothing to worry about. Simple as pie."

She broke off with a cough. "Sorry," she said. "Kronis is a little tough on the vocal cords. Must be a baritone."

"I'll get you some water," Pru said quickly. But I was already on my feet. "Be right back," I said, and headed for the kitchen.

I pushed open the swinging door and stopped. The sports section was spread out over the kitchen table. Zee and Cam sat at the table, eating waffles. They both looked up.

"Hi," I said. "I just came in to get a glass of water. For your mother."

Cam's blue eyes flickered over me. Then he looked back at the newspaper. "Help yourself," he said. "The glasses are next to the sink."

"She must be channeling," Zee remarked. She seemed to have gotten over her non-verbal phase.

"Yes," I said. I went to the sink and filled a glass with water. "It was very interesting."

"Which one was it this time?" Zee asked.

"Kronis," I said. "The Druid one."

"Oh, him." She rolled her eyes. "Bor-ing," she said. She took a bite of waffle and chewed it languidly.

I watched Cam studying the sports page. "I heard you might be going to our school," I said, smiling nervously. "I think you'll really like it."

He was still reading the paper. When nobody answered, he looked up. "Oh, yeah?" he said. "Does it have a swimming pool?"

I blinked. "A pool? No, but . . ."

Cam turned back to the paper. "Back home our school had an Olympic-sized pool," he said. "Heated."

"Well, I'm afraid ours doesn't." I could feel the blood rising in my face. "But you could always go sit in your hot tub. If you got homesick for a heated pool, I mean."

There was a long silence while Cam and Zee stared at me. My chest felt tight, as if something was squeezing all the breath out of me. I couldn't believe I'd been so rude.

Then Zee began to laugh. "Hey, that's a good one," she said. "She's right, Cameroon. You can always go sit in the hot tub." She gave her brother a nudge, and he scowled at her.

I was blushing furiously. "I'm really sorry," I said. "I didn't mean—"

"Forget it." Folding the newspaper, Cam stood up, just as his mother burst into the kitchen.

"Come quick!" Chloe said, grabbing my arm. "Your sister has made contact with an Egyptian princess!"

Pru was sitting on the couch. Her eyes were shut,

and she swayed slowly from side to side. Chloe knelt beside her. "Speak to me, spirit of the Nile."

"I am the priestess Mara, daughter of the Great Pharaoh," Pru chanted. "We are the keepers of the Temple of the Sacred Cat. Tell me what you desire to know."

I stifled a groan. Just last week I'd shown Pru a library book about Egypt. I had even pointed out a picture of a mummified cat, and we'd laughed, picturing poor Winston bandaged up to his ears.

Zee and Cam were standing in the doorway, staring at Pru. Pru must have sensed them too, because she announced, "The channel is growing faint. I must leave before I cause her harm. But I will come again, with many things to tell . . . to teach . . ." Her voice faded off.

After a moment, Chloe touched Pru's arm. "It's okay, she's gone. You can come back now."

She turned to me. "What did you say her name was? I'm sorry, it's just so hard to tell you guys apart."

"It's Prune," I said helpfully. "That's short for Prunehilda."

Pru's face gave a twitch. "I'm . . . okay now," she murmured. "What happened?"

"You just channeled, Prune! First time out!" Chloe exclaimed. "And an Egyptian princess, no less."

Pru gazed around the room. "Really?"

I wanted to laugh. But Cam looked impressed.

"What was it like?" he asked. "Did you get dizzy or sick or anything? Or did you just kind of black out?"

Pru paused. "I guess I just kind of blacked out," she said. "And then, when it was over, I felt like I was really far away . . . like at the end of a long tunnel or something."

Cam nodded. He perched on the arm of the couch. "I've read about that," he said. "It happens when people come back from the dead."

Chloe was beaming at Pru. "See? I knew you were spiritually gifted, Prune. It must be a product of your twin aura." She turned to me. "I bet you guys use all sorts of ESP with each other."

"Oh, yes," I said. I glared at Pru. "In fact, I'm sending her a message right now. Can you read it, Princess Mara?"

"Princess who?" Pru said.

"Mara," Cam informed her. "That's the Egyptian spirit who was speaking through you."

He glanced at me. Then he looked back at Pru, and shook his head. "That's definitely spooky," he said. "Two people with the same face."

"And the same voice," Chloe added. "Oh, it must be such fun! I've always wanted to have a twin."

Cam leaned forward. "I read about these twins once," he began. "One of them said he could feel the actual incision when the other guy was having an operation." He looked at us again. "That ever happen to you?"

"No," I said.

"Oh, yes," Pru answered. She turned to me wide-eyed. "Remember that time you cut your foot, and I started limping, even though I didn't know you'd hurt yourself?"

"No," I said.

"Oh, it happens all the time," Pru assured him.

I looked around the room. Everyone was eating up Pru's phony twin stories, just like they'd bought her Princess Mara act. It made me sick.

"I forgot your water," I told Chloe, and hurried off to the kitchen.

The glass of water was still on the table. I picked it up and stood listening to Cam's lecture. He was holding forth with more amazing twin stories—twins who were separated at birth but ended up marrying people with the same first name, twins who played on the same basketball team and scored the same number of points for the season. He seemed to be quite an expert.

And then, as I listened, a depressing thought struck me. Cam and Chloe didn't care that I wrote poetry, or was going to be a famous artist someday. They weren't dying to hear how Pru had won the perfect penmanship award two years in a row, while my handwriting was a messy scrawl.

All people ever wanted to hear were the spooky twin stories. They weren't interested in what was different about us, only what was the same.

Personally, I never wanted to hear another amazing

twin story as long as I lived. Pru and I didn't play basketball, and we weren't going to marry people with the same name. And as for getting separated at birth, it was too late now. I wondered if twins ever got separated in junior high. I doubted it, but it was a nice thought.

Cam was still lecturing away. I took a deep breath and pushed open the kitchen door.

As I handed Chloe the water, Cam looked up with a smile. "So," he asked, "how do your parents tell you two apart?"

I glanced at Pru. She was still sitting on the couch, recovering from her trance.

I looked back at Cam. "By our eyebrows," I said.

five

~~~~~~

"Mattie? Would you pass me the last chocolate dough-nut?" Heather said. "Unless you want it," she added.

It was the inaugural meeting of the 2 + 1 Club, Pru's latest brainstorm. It didn't take a genius to figure out what the 2 + 1 stood for.

At least it was a good excuse for some decent refreshments. I was getting pretty tired of digging stale Mars bars out of the sofa. I reached for the doughnuts we had smuggled in under Sally's nose.

"You can have it, Heather. Unless Princess Mara would like it. Or should I say, *Prune*-cess Mara?"

"Cut it out, Mattie!" Pru snatched the doughnut off the plate and handed it to Heather. All weekend we'd been wrangling over the famous channeling episode. Pru complained that everyone kept calling her Prune. Chloe, she said, even asked how our parents had come up with the unusual name of Prunehilda.

"Why would people named Chloe and Zoe think Prunehilda was unusual?" I asked.

"That's not the point! The point is, I had to keep telling them my name is not Prune. Anyway, it's not my fault I had a genuine out-of-the-body experience. You act as though I made the whole thing up. Just so you could punish me with that awful name!"

"Zee calls her brother Cameroon," I pointed out.

"Anybody decide what to wear on the first day of school?" Heather asked, tactfully changing the subject. "I got a great sweater at Wyndham's. And pants to go with it."

"I don't want to think about sweaters or school yet," I said.

"Well, I don't want to think about teachers and classes," Pru sighed.

Heather shrugged. "I don't really mind homework. In a weird way, I've kind of missed it."

"Well, you're the studious type," I told her. That was putting it mildly. Heather was the main brain at Puget Sound. She even got A's in Latin, a subject that only brains like Heather were allowed to take.

"At least we'll have some new faces in the hall," I added, munching on a doughnut. "If you know what I mean."

"What's he like?" Heather asked, picking chocolate crumbs off the plate. "The new boy next door?"

"Utterly gorgeous, that's what he's like. And very athletic. Back at his old school, he was on the swimming and tennis teams," Pru reported.

"He seems kind of stuck up at first," I said. "But he's

probably okay once you get to know him."

"Oh, how would you know, Mattie?" Pru burst out. "You're always judging people on first impressions. That's your trouble, you never give anybody a chance."

"That's not true! Just because I don't put on a big phony act to impress people doesn't mean—"

"Come on, you guys," Heather interrupted. "I just asked what he was like. I didn't mean to start World War III."

I glared at Pru. "Sorry, Heather," I said. "I guess you'll just have to find out for yourself."

But on the first day of school, Cam wasn't there.

"Maybe Lyle and Chloe decided not to send him to Puget Sound after all," I told Pru. She didn't say anything, but she looked crestfallen.

I tried to tell myself that it was just as well, that at least this way we'd avoid World War III. But deep down I felt pretty crestfallen too.

On Tuesday morning, I stopped at the school bulletin board. I was just trying to decide whether to submit some poetry to the school literary magazine, *The Puget Sound Parthenon*, when I heard a familiar voice coming from the principal's office.

"Thank you so much," Chloe was saying. "I realize it's an inconvenience, enrolling him after school's already started. But we're just thrilled he'll be attending Puget Sound. And I'm personally looking forward to getting involved in your parent association. I guess you could say—"

"—I'm a people kind of person," I finished under my breath.

I had just finished re-reading a notice for tuba lessons when someone tapped me on the shoulder. Cam stood behind me, a brand new notebook tucked under the arm of his denim jacket.

"Hi," he said. "Listen, I got sick of sitting in that hot tub. Besides, my folks joined a health club with a heated pool. So I decided I'd better show up for class."

Then he peered at me. "Were you the one who was talking about pools? Or was that the other one?"

I was in the middle of laughing at his hot tub joke. I stopped laughing abruptly. "The name is Mattie," I said. "And yes, I recall discussing swimming pools." I turned away and pretended to study the bulletin board. "So how come you weren't here yesterday?" I asked.

Cam glanced down the hall. His mother was still talking to the school secretary. "Mom thought the stars were in the wrong aspect," he muttered.

"What?"

He looked pained. "Mom's into astrology. When she did my chart yesterday, she didn't think it checked out. Listen," he said in a rush, "it wasn't my idea. I don't believe in that stuff. But you know Mom."

"Maybe she was right," I said. "I mean, you can never be too careful. Besides," I added, "you didn't miss much. Just a boring assembly and a bunch of roll calls."

Cam nodded. Then he glanced at something on the bulletin board. "Hey, check this out."

He pointed to a poster. "Win a free racing bike!" it said in big red letters. "Or choose the latest fall fashions. Enter Wyndham's Department Store/Seattle Center art contest. First prize includes a $300 gift certificate from Wyndham's, plus free passes to events at the Center. Ride the Monorail, dine atop the Space Needle, and celebrate the anniversary of Seattle's World's Fair." In smaller letters, it said, "See your art teacher for details."

"Three hundred bucks, huh?" Cam said. He grinned at me. "Hey, maybe I just got good at art!"

The bell rang, and Cam glanced at his class schedule. "Catch you later," he said. "And listen, that was great the way you pulled off that Egyptian thing. My mom hasn't stopped talking about it."

I turned back to the bulletin board with a groan. What was the use? Cam Davis didn't have the faintest idea which twin was which. And the way things were going, he never would.

Then I realized I was staring at the poster for the Wyndham's contest. As I read it again, a little video began to play inside my head. I saw myself standing next to the winning display at Wyndham's. And I pictured Cam's face as I stepped up to accept my prize and graciously offered to share it with my deserving neighbor.

"I'm glad you're so good at art," he'd say as we rode

to the restaurant on top of the Space Needle. "Listen, there's a great horror movie playing at the Uptown Cinema. Maybe after dinner we could—"

The late bell rang, and I jumped. But the glorious images still gleamed before my eyes. As soon as gym was over, I decided, I'd head straight for the art room and apply.

In gym, Mrs. Schaefer had to fill in her yearly charts. Everyone got weighed and measured and had to run around the gym, climbing up ropes and jumping over the horse. None of it was too awful, but I felt sweaty and tired by the time I was dressed and headed for study hall.

As I started up the stairs, a hand grabbed my arm.

"Mattie, you've got to help me!" Pru stood clutching her French book, a look of anguish on her face.

"What is it? What's the matter?"

"I can't believe it! Heather just told me we're getting a quiz in French. The second day of school!" Pru flushed angrily. "There ought to be a law about stuff like that. It's not fair!"

"Why not?" I said. "Didn't you do the assignment we got yesterday?"

"Well . . ." Pru leaned against the green tiles that lined the stairwell. "Sort of. But I didn't think the old witch would be sticking us with a test so soon. I mean, it's only the second day of school!"

"You've pointed that out," I said, but my stomach

muscles tightened. Pru was about to ask for something.

"Do you think I could look at your notes, Mattie? Just this once? I know you did the assignment. I saw you studying it last night."

Relief swept over me. Pru and I were in different classes, and mine wasn't until after lunch. "Sorry, but I didn't take any notes," I said. "I don't have French until this afternoon, remember? Anyway, I figured I'd look at the chapter next period, in study hall."

I moved away from the wall, but Pru was right behind me.

"Oh, you've got a study period? But that's perfect! See, I could take your study hall and be all set for French. Which is . . ." She consulted the schedule taped to her notebook. "Fourth period. Oh, please, Mattie? After all, you've got early lunch today. You could study French then."

"But . . ." In spite of everything, I was starting to weaken.

Then Pru's plan sank in.

"But if you take my study period, that means I have to take . . ." I stared at her. "You don't expect me to . . ."

Pru gazed back patiently. "It's just gym. It's not like I'm asking you to do my homework, Mattie. Just pull your hair back. Schaefer will never know the difference."

A trickle of horror slid down my spine. "No," I said, knowing it wouldn't do any good. "I'm not going to impersonate you, Pru."

"Mattie," Pru said. "I'm not asking you to do anything I wouldn't do for you."

Standing on the stairs, I felt the force of Pru's will wash over me like a sticky tidal wave. For a moment I wondered if Chloe was right. Maybe Pru really did have supernatural powers. "But I just had gym," I said weakly.

"I'll make it up to you," Pru said quickly, somehow sensing she'd won. "You can borrow any of my clothes you want. For a whole week," she added. "And I'll never pick another fight with you again," she called, hurrying off to my study hall. "Thanks, Mattie!"

I leaned against the tiles like a fighter on the ropes and watched her disappear up the stairs. Hurricane Pru, I thought. Whoosh. I'd never stood a chance.

six

~~~~~~~~~~~~~~~~~~~~~~~~~~~~~~~~~~~~~

I sat very still and closed my eyes. As the school bus rattled up Queen Anne Hill, I listened to the kids laughing and talking around me, and tried not to think about my second gym class.

Instead, I remembered opening Pru's locker and putting on Pru's gym clothes. I watched myself pull my hair into a ponytail and walk out to the gym, where Mrs. Schaefer wrote down my height and weight again, only this time next to Pru's name. (Pru actually weighed a few pounds more, but Schaefer didn't know that.) The whole time I kept hoping someone would rush up and say, "Mattie? What on earth are *you* doing here?"

But no one said anything. By the end of class, I was a mess. I hated the way I felt—interchangeable. It was worse than being invisible.

The bus stopped. I opened my eyes and watched Pru and Heather get off the bus and head down the street together.

That was fine with me. Prunehilda was starting to give me the creeps. What would she make me do next? Pluck my eyebrows? Clean our room twice a day? Hypnotize me and turn me into her personal zombie?

Finally I got off the bus too and began to trudge down McIntire Street. A city bus pulled up at the corner, and Zee and Cam clambered off. Even from a distance, you could tell they were brother and sister, both of them tall and dark, wearing jeans and boys' shirts. The main difference was their hair — Cam's was thick and curly and normal-looking, but his sister's stuck up in weird pointed spikes. She looked like Bugsy, the Bakers' Airedale terrier, after he'd been out in the rain too long.

I tried to picture what the ladies down at the Cut 'n' Curl Salon would say about Zee's hair. "Quick, girls!" Blanche, who did the manicures, would shout. "I'll hold her down, while the rest of you give her a permanent!" Old Zee would come out looking like Little Orphan Annie.

And then, as I watched her spikes turn in at the Davises' house, a brilliant idea suddenly zipped into my head. It was so simple, I couldn't imagine why I'd never thought of it before.

I began to hurry down the street. I couldn't wait to tell Heather. If this worked the way I hoped it would, even Cam would be able to remember my name.

Especially Cam.

I loved going to Heather's house. It was the same size as ours, but the rooms seemed bigger and brighter. The windows sparkled, there were vases full of flowers, and the floors were made of shiny golden wood that always smelled like lemons.

Heather's mom worked for an import business, so the house was full of stuff from places like India and Thailand. My favorites were the huge paper fish that hung in the front hall. Every time you opened the door, the fish swam down from the ceiling and bobbed at you, as if they were trying to say hello.

Mrs. Yamamoto answered the doorbell. I silently greeted the fish and took an appreciative sniff of lemon polish. "Hi," I said. "Is Heather upstairs?"

Mrs. Yamamoto must have just gotten home from work, because she was wearing one of her tiny, elegant suits. It was dark red with black piping around the collar and cuffs. Probably a size one. I couldn't take my eyes off it.

"Your sister was just here." she said, whisking me into the hall with a smile. "I invited her in, but she said she had to get right home."

"She probably wanted to get started on her homework," I said. Sure, I thought. While she kept one eye out the window for stray Davises.

Mrs. Yamamoto nodded brightly. She was very big on people doing their homework. That was probably one reason Heather was such a brain. Personally, I figured it was also why Heather spent more and more time in her room studying, and less time having any fun.

But I never said anything. When it was time to apply for college, riding your bike and going to the mall probably wouldn't count for much. Even so, no one should have to study *all* the time.

"Is it okay if I go upstairs?" I asked politely. All the Yamamotos were very polite, and it kind of rubbed off on a person. Temporarily, as my mother liked to point out.

"Yes, of course." Mrs. Yamamoto smiled. "Heather's just changing her clothes. But please tell her she has to get in some practicing before dinner."

"Okay." I took one last look at the red-and-black suit, wondering how much kelp a person would have to consume to shrink down to a size one. Then I sped up the stairs to Heather's room.

She stood in front of her closet, pulling a sweatshirt over her head. "Guess what?" I said, bouncing down on the bed. "I've come to a momentous decision." And I told her about my brilliant plan.

"You're *what*?"

"I'm going to get my hair cut."

Heather fingered her long, shiny hair. "Do you mean cut," she asked, "or just trimmed?"

I looked at my reflection in the mirror. "I mean, I'm going to get my hair cut. Off!"

Heather wrinkled her nose. "You're not going to end

up looking like a marine recruit or something, are you?"

"Of course not," I said. "But it's got to be really short and, well, distinctive."

"Couldn't you just buy some new clothes?" she suggested. "You have such pretty hair, Mattie. Maybe you could get a perm instead." Besides being literal-minded, Heather isn't the most adventurous person in the world.

"No," I said firmly, "it's all or nothing. I've thought this over, and it's absolutely the only way I can establish my own identity. I can't be a clone forever."

"Well, okay," Heather said, but she didn't sound very convinced. "So where are you going to get it cut?"

I paused. My brilliant plan hadn't exactly covered that point. There was the Gene Juarez Salon, where the rich and famous went, or at least the people who wanted to look rich and famous. But their prices were pretty much out of my range. The only other place I could think of was the Cut 'n' Curl Salon.

I pictured Blanche. Forget the Cut 'n' Curl.

"What difference does it make?" I said. "The main thing is to do it soon. Before I change my mind."

Heather nodded. "There's this girl in my homeroom—Lydia Carthage. She just got her hair cut. Maybe you could ask her."

Things were looking up, I thought. I had a plan, I had an ally, and in my wallet was the twenty-dollar bill

Grandma Bradshaw had sent each of us on our last birthday. "Thanks, Heather," I said. "Maybe I will."

Then I paused. "Just one more thing. Don't say anything to Pru, okay? Until, you know, it's over."

Heather was silent. I began to feel nervous. Maybe I shouldn't have said anything. After all, Heather was Pru's best friend too. Sometimes things just slipped out.

Then Heather smiled. "Don't worry, Mattie. I won't say a word. Hey, you want to hear the new song I'm learning?"

Heather reached for her violin case, and I reached for a pillow. Wrapping the pillow around both ears, I lay back on the bed to picture my glorious non-identical future. No one would ever call me Pru again. People wouldn't suddenly go cross-eyed when they saw us together. And Cam—

My thoughts were shattered by a blast of music. I looked at Heather, but her bow was still poised over her violin. A second later, we heard the bellowing of a slightly off-key tenor.

Mr. Yamamoto was home.

The next day, I stationed myself outside Heather's homeroom. When the bell rang, Heather pointed to a tall blond girl who was walking toward the door.

The minute she reached the hall, I pounced.

"Lydia? Hi, my name's Mattie, and my friend Heather said you might know of a good place to get my hair cut." I paused to catch my breath and check out

Lydia's hair. It was cropped close to her head, except for some short wisps around her face. It looked very fashionable.

Lydia stared at me. "Sorry," she said. "I had this done in Paris. I'm afraid I wouldn't know of any place around here."

She gave me a long look that took in my rumpled shirt and my scuffed shoes. "Maybe you could find something in the Yellow Pages," Lydia said, smiling thinly. Then she moved off down the crowded hall.

Heather hurried over. "Well? Did she tell you where to go?"

I was staring after Lydia. "Yes," I said. "As a matter of fact, I think she did."

When lunchtime came, I gathered up my courage and marched over to the ninth-grade table. Two minutes later, I reported back to Heather.

"They all said the same thing. A place called the Animal Cage on First Avenue."

Heather nodded. Then we both clammed up as Pru sat down with her lunch tray. I picked up my sandwich and tried to eat, but my stomach was jumping up and down. In a few more hours, my life as an identical nobody—a Darwin clone—would be over.

After lunch, I headed straight for the art room. The contest rules were posted next to the blackboard. I read through them quickly. The theme of the contest was "Explore a Wonderland in Your Own Backyard." The wonders included the Repertory Theater, the

Opera House, the Monorail, the Pacific Science Center, and, of course, the Space Needle.

The contest was open to every junior high in the city. According to the rules, you could do any kind of project you wanted, from a poster or collage to a full-scale model, but it had to tie in with the Center's anniversary celebration.

Then I saw that the deadline was the last week in September. That wouldn't give me much time. Not if I was going to win.

I grabbed an entry form off the stack on Mr. Gruenfeld's desk and scribbled my name. Then I hurried out of the room and up the stairs to math, the only class I shared with Pru.

Putting us in different classes was Sally's idea. She claimed we would make more friends and "develop stronger social skills." In my opinion, it had only made things worse.

There must be some law of nature, I thought, as I slipped into the desk next to Pru's. The minute people found out you were a twin, they could never remember your name, even if you sat in front of them for a whole year. Our parents should have just named us both Pru. It would have saved everyone a lot of trouble.

Pru leaned over and poked me.

"If you want me to impersonate you in this class, forget it," I said. "They'll never go for it."

"Listen," Pru said, "I think we should go over to

Chloe's after school. We could bring Heather—you know, let her meet Cam and everything."

"I can't," I said. "There's some stuff I have to do at the library. Heather's going to help me," I added, trying to ignore the black look that had crossed Pru's face.

"What stuff?" she demanded. "Why can't I come?"

"It's just homework," I said, hoping I didn't sound as desperate as I felt. "Some stuff Mrs. Carlson wanted us to look up for English."

Pru studied me suspiciously. Then she shrugged. "Fine," she said. "I'll go visit Chloe by myself."

"Have a good time," I told her as Mr. Garofalo walked into the room. "Say hi to Princess Mara for me," I added.

Mr. Garofalo tapped on his desk, and we plunged into the wonderful world of time and distance problems. But I could feel Pru's eyes boring into me the whole time.

For the rest of the day, I tried not to check the clock more than four times an hour. Finally, the last bell rang, and I ran down to the side entrance, where Heather was waiting. Together, we set off in search of the Animal Cage.

First Avenue was down by the city waterfront. New shops and restaurants were starting to spring up, but the long blocks were still full of seedy magazine stores and pawn shops. A group of disheveled men lounged at the Union Street bus stop, drinking wine from a brown paper bag and spitting into the street. They stared at us as we hurried past.

"Is this a good idea, Mattie?" Heather said nervously. "My mom would kill me if she knew we were down here."

"Come on," I said, trying to sound braver than I felt. "It's just a few more blocks."

We passed the Public Market, looking for the Animal Cage. Then Heather grabbed my arm. "Look," she said. "There it is."

I could see where they got the name. Bars covered the windows, which were filled with exotic plants and ferns. Then the door of the Animal Cage opened, and someone wearing a leather jacket decorated with a skull and crossbones stepped outside and lit a cigarette. The person—I couldn't tell if it was male or female—threw back its mass of black curls and gave us a hostile stare before sauntering down First Avenue.

I touched the wallet where my grandmother's twenty dollars was tucked between my library card and junior lifesaving badge. For a moment I considered catching a bus to the nearest beauty parlor, where someone a lot like my grandmother could give me a nice, simple pixie cut.

Then I thought of Pru babbling about ancient Egypt while Cam stared at her adoringly. "Come on," I told Heather. I opened the door.

Inside, a red-haired girl wearing an Animal Cage T-shirt sat behind an ornate desk. "Yes?" she said.

I glanced at Heather and stepped up to the desk. "I'd like to get my hair cut."

The girl pursed her lips. "Today? Do you have an appointment?"

I looked around the salon. There were animals everywhere—stuffed ones, painted ones, wooden ones. In the corner a green parrot suddenly let out a scream and began to scratch itself with one foot.

Behind a bank of plants, a row of stylists snipped and swooped to the sound of deafening music. Nearby, a boy about our age was asleep in a chair, his head covered with tiny strips of aluminum foil.

"Well, no," I told the girl. "But . . ."

The appointment girl looked cross. Then she sighed and checked her list.

"Oh, all right," she said finally. "I can give you to Ramon. Ramon!" she called above the screaming parrot and the booming sound system. "You've got a walk-in."

Two minutes later, I sat perched in an antique dental chair, staring at myself in a wall of mirrors. Ramon, who was young and muscular and had bright yellow hair, stared into the mirror too.

He picked up the ends of my hair and flipped them between his fingers. "I hope," he sighed, "this is all going to go?"

"Oh, yes," I assured him. I checked the mirror to make sure Heather was still waiting for me in the outer Cage. "I'd like it very short. But distinctive."

Sitting there in the dentist's chair, I suddenly wished I'd brought a picture from a magazine or maybe a sketch—something to show Ramon I didn't want to end up looking like a cross between Zee Davis and a marine.

Instead, I tried to describe the look I had in mind. But as my voice went on and on, I realized I was describing Lydia Carthage.

Ramon stepped back to study my hair. His lips compressed and his nostrils pinched. He looked as though he had just bitten into a rotten peanut.

Then, with a sudden burst of energy, he snatched up a handful of hair clips and a pair of scissors.

"Yes," he murmured. "I think I know just what we want. And don't worry," he added, vigorously spritzing my head with a plant mister. "I just know we're going to love it!"

seven

~~~~~~

On the ride back to Queen Anne, Heather and I compared notes about the Animal Cage.

In my opinion, the second-worst moment came when I went to pay for the haircut, and the girl told me it was forty-five dollars. Heather agreed that was pretty bad, especially when I pulled out my twenty-dollar bill with "Happy Birthday!" written on it and told the receptionist that was all the money I had. She muttered something about walk-ins, but she took the twenty dollars.

For Heather, the worst moment was when the boy next to me had the foil taken out of his hair. He looked at the mirror and started to scream. The parrot in the corner started screaming too. "But I thought you *wanted* to go red," the stylist kept saying, as the boy clutched at his head. "Go red! Go red!" said the parrot.

Finally I had to admit that the very worst moment of

all was when Ramon stopped snipping and spraying and tweaking at my hair. He put down his spritzer and pointed at the mirror. "Well?" he asked proudly. "Do we love it?"

Slowly I lifted my eyes. A strange-looking girl stared back at me. The girl had reddish-brown hair, just like mine. But that was where the resemblance ended.

Actually, there was hardly enough hair to tell what color it was. It was slicked down with some shiny stuff, except for the top, which stuck up in stiff, pointed peaks. Poor girl, I thought. She looked just like a cross between Zee Davis and a marine.

When the bus finished climbing the hill, we got off and stood in front of Heather's house.

"I think your hair looks very nice," Heather said, but I could tell she was just being a polite Yamamoto. "Even if you don't like it, it'll grow out."

"No, I like it. A lot," I said. This was what I would tell people, I decided. Maybe if I pretended I liked it, I wouldn't feel so stupid. "It's just what I wanted."

Then I hurried off before Mrs. Yamamoto caught sight of me and called the cops.

When I got home, I paused at the front door. I reached up and touched my strange new hair. The stiff peaks had dried hard in the afternoon sun. What was left felt like clipped, matted duck feathers.

Disappointment settled over me like a heavy blanket. Cutting my hair had seemed like such a great idea yesterday. But I didn't feel any different, except that now I looked a whole lot worse. And I wondered what Pru was going to say.

I crept upstairs and peeked in our room. It was empty. The Princess Mara Family Hour must still be in session.

"Mattie? Is that you?"

My father stood in the hall, gazing at me curiously. Sometimes my mom got us mixed up, especially if she'd had a long day. But not Dad. Even if I were wearing a gorilla suit, dancing the tango, and smoking a cigar, my father would still know it was me and not Pru. I never asked him how he knew, and I didn't ask him now.

"I got my hair cut," I said.

"Yes," he said. He stroked his beard thoughtfully. "You did indeed. It's very . . . different."

"I know." I paused. "It's awful, isn't it."

My father studied my spiky head for a moment. Then he smiled. "Seeing as how I've survived a lot more bad haircuts than you have," he said, "I'll let you in on a little secret. Don't pass judgment until you've stuck your head under the water faucet. It'll still look short, but at least you'll recognize yourself." He patted me on the shoulder. "Trust me."

With another encouraging pat, my father walked down the hall to his study. I heard him chuckling to himself as he closed the door.

I paused only a second before racing to the bathroom. Turning on the cold water, I let the gel and glue that Ramon had plastered on my hair wash away. When my hair felt clean again, I rubbed it with a towel. Then I looked in the mirror.

The girl who looked back still had very short hair, but at least the weird peaks were gone. Curling my fingers, I drew them lightly through my short, wet hair. I shook my head, and the cold tips of hair whipped at my ears.

Then I looked at myself again, and for a second I couldn't believe my eyes. It was really true, I thought. I didn't look like Prunehilda anymore. I looked like . . . *me.*

" 'Beaton, tell them I am ready,' Mary instructed her servant. 'Hush, now, there is no reason to weep. Come, Beaton, we must go to my death serenely.' "

I was hunched on the bed, trying to get through the last five-and-a-half inches of *Mary, Queen of Scots.* The next time I did a summer project, I was definitely going to pick short stories.

In the meantime, reading them aloud in a crisp English accent seemed to make the boring parts more interesting. Plus it was easier to imagine you were Queen Mary, about to get your head chopped off, but being English and gracious about it right up to the last second.

There was a tap on the door. "Dinner will be ready in ten minutes, Your Majesty," Sally called.

Thank you, Darwin, I thought. That will be all.

"Okay," I called back. Where, I wondered, was Pru? I thought about running next door and making a dramatic entrance. But then I decided the casual approach would be much more effective.

"Hi, Cam," I'd say, strolling past him in the hall.

"Mattie? Mattie Darwin? Wow, I'd never have recognized you. You look so different—and well, great—with that new haircut."

"Just thought I'd try something new," I would answer modestly. "Besides, short hair is much more convenient for things like tennis. Or swimming."

"We'll have the hot tub hooked up soon," Cam would say. "Then you and the other one can come over and try it out."

"Her name's Pru," I'd answer loyally. "But thank you. That really sounds—"

The bedroom door flew open. "Mom says to get down . . ."

Pru stopped and stared at me. "Mattie?" Her voice quivered. "What . . . what have you done?"

I put a hand up to my hair. "Do you like it?"

Pru opened her mouth. Then she shut it again. She stood there like a giant goldfish, opening and shutting her mouth. After a moment, she walked over to the bed.

"Why didn't you tell me you were getting your hair cut?" Pru's voice was thick and accusing. "You didn't have to make up a big story about going to the library!"

"I wanted it to be a surprise."

"It's a surprise, all right," Pru said. "I just can't believe you'd do something like this and not tell me!"

I put down my book. "To tell you the truth, I was afraid you'd try to talk me out of it."

Pru perched gingerly on the bed, as though I had some contagious disease. "Of course I would have tried to talk you out of it!" she said. "Now we're not twins anymore."

"Don't be stupid," I said. "We're still twins. We'll *always* be twins."

"But we won't look like twins," Pru stated.

I sighed. "That was the whole point, Pru. I didn't want to look like a twin anymore. I wanted to look like *me*."

Pru frowned. "Why?" she asked in a puzzled voice.

I rolled over on my side and glanced across the room. A big mirror hung above our dresser at the exact point where the wallpaper met. Three years ago, when we picked out the wallpaper for our room, Pru had just seen the movie *National Velvet*, so she chose a pattern of brown horses jumping over white fences. I picked a paisley design called "Royal Regency." The total effect was pretty hideous, but since we never got around to wallpapering again, we were stuck with it.

In the mirror I could see Pru and me framed by brown horses on one side and red-and-green paisley on the other. That was us in a nutshell, I thought—stuck side by side and clashing hopelessly, but never getting any closer.

Then I flashed on something else. "Remember?" I said. "How we used to have those Who's Prettier contests?"

They'd started in third grade. Pru and I would stand in front of the mirror and compare features, scoring points for each flaw we could find in the other twin.

"I'm prettier, because you have more freckles on your nose," Pru would say.

"No, *I'm* prettier, because your eyes are closer together."

"You've got that mole on your cheek."

"But your bottom teeth are crooked."

We never figured out who was prettier. But maybe, I thought, as I stared at our reflections, that wasn't the point. Maybe even back in the third grade, we just needed to make sure we were different.

Pru smiled faintly, and I hoped the shock of my hair-cut was wearing off. "That was your idea," she said. "You got all worked up when you found that dumb mole on your face."

"You were the one who found it," I reminded her. "Besides, it was your idea. Because of the time you fell downstairs and your tooth came in crooked."

"That's right, I forgot about that."

We looked at each other. "It's kind of cute," Pru said finally. "Your hair."

"You should have seen it a few hours ago. I looked just like Zee Davis." I paused. "So how did your visit go?"

Pru shrugged. "Cam was off playing tennis. Chloe talked about Mom's restaurant the whole time, and made me drink about a million kiwi sparklers while she told me every recipe for octopus ever invented."

That was when my mother poked her head in the room. "Dinner's ready," she said.

Her eyes slid past me. Then they slid back. "Cute haircut," she remarked. "But I wish you girls had done that at the beginning of the summer. It would have been so much cooler that way."

As soon as she was gone, I burst out laughing. A second later, Pru started laughing too. Being twins, we have the same laugh, a weird cackle that sounds like twin hens laying twin eggs. Listening to us cackle, I wondered why we couldn't always get along like this. The way we used to.

Finally Pru stopped laughing. She stood up. "I'll probably get used to your hair," she said. "But I don't see why you couldn't have told me."

I hesitated. "Actually, I was afraid you'd want to get yours cut too."

I guess it was the wrong thing to say. Pru's shoulders stiffened, and her face turned bright red.

"You thought I'd want to get mine cut too?" Pru glared at me. "You honestly think I'd run out and get a crew cut, just so we could still be twins? Give me a break, Mattie! That's so totally pathetic, I can't believe it!"

"Come on, Pru . . ." I said nervously. But she was already stomping out of the room.

I sat on the bed and listened to Pru's footsteps thud down the stairs. By the time she reached the bottom step, it began to dawn on me what was really bothering her.

It wasn't my hair at all. It was something a whole lot worse: The Normie Zone.

Normies. That was what we used to call the non-twins—half out of pity, but partly from envy too. Staring at myself in the mirror, I didn't blame Pru for being scared. Becoming a normie at our advanced age was a pretty scary thought.

All the same, I could hardly wait.

eight

~~~~~~~~~~~~~~~~~~~~~~~~~~~~~~~~~~~~~~~

As we walked into school the next day, I braced myself for the reaction to the new me.

I was still bracing myself by the time we stood at our lockers. A few kids glanced at us, but nobody screamed. Nobody fainted. Nobody said anything at all.

"Stunned silence," I told Pru. "They're probably still in shock."

Pru gave me a sour smile. Then she moved off to her homeroom and I finished putting my books away. I was hunting through my bag for a comb when Mr. Garofalo strolled out of the math room. He saw me and smiled.

"Hi, Pru," he said. "Did you have any trouble with those homework problems? You looked a little confused yesterday."

"No, sir," I mumbled. "No trouble at all."

With a cheerful nod, he walked back into his room.

I found my comb and yanked it through what was

left of my hair. For the millionth time I wondered why people thought being a twin would be so great. On one hand, you got loads of attention for something you'd had nothing to do with. On the other hand, no one ever called you by the right name. It would drive any normie nuts within a week.

"So much for my brilliant idea," I told Heather. We sat in the lunchroom, poking our forks into the daily special, Mystery Meat au Gratin. I stared gloomily at a lone pea that had found its way into the sauce. "I should have let Ramon talk me into going red. Or redder, anyway. Then someone might have noticed my hair."

"They noticed, Mattie," Heather said loyally. "Marcia Ames thought your hair looked really cute. She wanted to know if Pru was going to get hers cut too."

I groaned. "See? That just proves it! Once a Darwin clone, always one. I could legally change my name to Godzilla, and Mr. Garofalo would still call me Pru!"

"Come on," Heather said. "This stuff takes time. People will notice you're different. You've just got to give them a chance."

But the only person I wanted to give that chance to wasn't around. Chloe must have seen something in his chart.

Maybe I should stop by on my way home. "The Druid Appreciation Society is meeting at school next Wednesday," I could tell Chloe. "We'd love it if you—and Kronis—could be our guest speakers."

"Lyle! Cam!" Chloe would scream. "Look, it's one of the twins. And she has the most adorable haircut!" Then I would smile modestly as they assembled to admire the vibrant new me.

Picturing that cheered me up a little. In the meantime, I still had to come up with a project for the contest.

Maybe I could do something on the Monorail, I thought, as I stepped up to get a library pass. I loved the Monorail. I wished it went all over the city instead of just the short distance between the Westlake Mall and the Center. I was busy picturing Seattle connected by a huge monorail network as I turned the corner and started toward the school library.

Then I stopped. A few yards away, Cam stood in front of the patriotic poster display outside the library. He was talking to Lydia Carthage.

So much for the Druid Appreciation Society. Gripping my notebook, I walked toward them.

Lydia saw me first. As I reached the patriotic poster display, her face sort of froze, as if I'd just stepped out of a flying saucer.

I came to a stop in front of Cam. "Hi!" I said.

"Hi," Cam said. He was staring at me too.

I gave him a friendly smile. "So," I went on, "been doing much swimming lately? You know—ha ha—at the health club?" My voice shook, but I forged ahead.

"I keep telling my parents that we ought to join. I've always wanted to take up tennis. That is . . ."

Cam was shifting from foot to foot. "Tennis, huh?" He adjusted his books under his arm and glanced at Lydia.

I wished she would go away. Cam probably wanted to say something about my hair, about how different I looked. But he wasn't going to do that with good old Lydia hanging around like the plague.

She kept darting little looks at Cam. All of a sudden she leaned forward and peered at me.

"Why, it's one of the Twinkies." Her voice sounded amused and grown-up. "Your hair looks adorable."

She heaved a big phony sigh. "Gee, if I'd known you could get a decent haircut here in Seattle, I wouldn't have had to go all the way to Paris."

I scowled at her, but Cam turned with a look of admiration. "Really? All the way to Paris?"

"Sure, whenever I want. My dad's an airline pilot," Lydia explained. "I've been practically all over the world."

"That must be great," Cam said.

Lydia smiled. She looked like a big blond lizard, I thought, basking in the sun after swallowing a bug. "I'd love to tell you about it," she said, "but I have to get to home ec. We're baking pies today."

"Pies," Cam repeated. I pictured a great big pie with

Lydia inside it, slowly suffocating as the crust covered her head.

She moved lightly down the hall. "Bye, Cam. Bye, Twinkie," she called. "Love the hair," she added over her shoulder.

Cam stared after her. "Paris," he said. "Wouldn't that be outrageous?"

"Yeah," I said. "Outrageous."

"Well . . ." He hoisted his books with an apologetic smile. "Gotta go. See ya around."

"Yeah, see ya."

I walked slowly into the library and sat down at one of the wooden study tables. Cam hadn't said anything about my hair; he hadn't even noticed it. And it was all because of horrible Lydia and her horrible father, the airline pilot. Right then, I made a vow never to fly anywhere again, not even to visit my grandmother in San Diego. I'd have to check if there were any trains to San Diego. Or buses. Or maybe—

"You're one of the Darwin twins, aren't you?"

I looked up. A tall thin boy was picking magazines off the table and putting them in a pile. He had long black hair that he kept tossing out of his eyes with a nervous flick of his head. But he was smiling at me in a friendly way. I nodded.

"I see you finally broke the mold. Good for you."

When I looked mystified, the boy grinned. "Your hair," he said. "It looks good on you. A little short on top, but I guess that's what passes for fashion nowadays."

I smiled uncertainly. I couldn't tell if he was making fun of me or not.

Then the boy looked embarrassed. "I'm sorry," he said. "You probably think I'm some kind of lunatic, handing you my personal opinions on your hair and—"

He broke off and glanced at Mrs. Bargreen, the librarian. "I'm the library assistant," he said, flicking his head again. "As a result, I know everybody in school, but no one's too sure about me."

"I know who you are," I told him. "You check the video equipment out for health class sometimes. You're . . ."

"Nelson. Nelson Richfield," the boy said. "And you're Mattie Darwin, aren't you? I used to sit behind you in English. You did a good book report on *Oliver Twist*, I thought. A little long-winded, but you made some interesting points."

That was when Mrs. Bargreen walked up behind us. "Nelson, please speak more quietly. Don't bother"— she glanced at me—"the girl here. Now, dear, do you need any help finding materials?"

"Actually," I said quickly, "I was just asking Nelson about some books on the history of Seattle. For a project I'm researching."

Nelson didn't miss a beat. "Yes, and I was about to show Mattie where she could find them."

"Good," Mrs. Bargreen said. She gazed at Nelson sternly, but there was a twinkle in her eye. "Just try to keep your voice down, Nelson. Others are trying to study."

"Yes, Mrs. B.," he muttered. She moved off toward her desk, and Nelson flashed me a grin. "Nice move, Darwin. I could tell she was about to blast me. She loves to do that." He sighed. "It gives her a sense of power, I think."

I peered at Nelson. He certainly was weird, I thought. But smart. And he didn't have any trouble remembering my name.

"I really did come in here to work on a project," I said, remembering to keep my voice down in case Mrs. Bargreen felt a power surge coming on. "It's for that contest sponsored by Wyndham's. I thought if I looked at some old books on Seattle, I might come up with an idea."

Nelson frowned. Something seemed to flash behind his eyes, and he reached up to give his hair a thoughtful push. Then he looked back at me, and a slow smile spread across his face.

"What?" I asked nervously. "What is it?"

"Dinosaurs," Nelson said. He looked smug. "Don't forget, you heard it here first."

The bell rang, signaling the end of last period. Doors banged, and a stampede of feet thundered down the hall toward the buses. I stared at Nelson. "Dinosaurs?" I said.

"Right," Nelson answered. "And if I have anything to say about it, Wyndham's will be ready to hand you the whole store, Mattie Darwin!"

Still wearing a secretive smile, Nelson Richfield collected his books and headed for the library door. Numbly, I followed.

nine

~~~~~~

"I don't get it," I said. "What do dinosaurs have to do with anything?"

We were standing in front of the school. A few feet away, Pru was waiting for the bus with Heather. From time to time, she shot Nelson a look of intense disapproval.

"You want to win this thing, right?" Nelson said. "Well, in my experience, people who win contests have strategies. And, because you saved me from the wrath of Mrs. B., I'm willing to give you a strategy that will accomplish certain goals."

His voice took on the professional-lecturer tone my father used when he was explaining the importance of the Industrial Revolution.

"One." Nelson gave his head an emphatic toss. "Your project must have visual appeal. Two." His eyes bored into me. "It must have an imaginative and informative subject. And three, it has to tie in with the contest theme."

I peered over my shoulder in case Pru was listening. "It's that last one I don't understand. Why dinosaurs?"

Nelson smiled inscrutably. "We'll get to that. But first we have to take care of one and two. And I figure dinosaurs are just the ticket. They're awesome, they're cute, and they've been dead for sixty-five million years." He grinned. "So they pose absolutely no danger to society. And they're definitely in the public domain."

A battered station wagon pulled up across the street. Nelson's narrow shoulders gave a twitch. "There's my mother," he said. "Now, don't worry, Darwin. We've got a winner here. In matters of importance, I am never wrong."

I watched him dash across the street and climb into the station wagon. Then the school bus rounded the corner, and I joined the other kids waiting to get on.

I headed for the backseat, but Pru was right behind me. "What was that all about?" she demanded. "You and what's-his-name?"

I flopped down next to the window. "His name is Nelson Richfield. He was just giving me a homework assignment."

"I thought maybe you were telling him where he could get a haircut," Pru said. "He could definitely use one."

I shrugged. "You're the one who told me not to judge people on first impressions."

Pru looked annoyed. "Maybe so, Mattie. But you have to admit he's kind of weird."

"So what?" I hunched down and stared deliberately out at the traffic. "I can talk to anyone I want," I said. But I said it under my breath.

And then, as the bus turned down Denny Way, a flash of color caught my eye. Hanging above the entrance to the Pacific Science Center was a big red banner. In yellow letters it announced: DINO DAYS— VISIT OUR LIFE-SIZED, ROARING, ANIMATED DINOSAURS IN THE MAIN EXHIBITION HALL. ON NOW THROUGH DECEMBER.

I stared at the banner rippling in the breeze. I felt like the very first amphibian who'd peered out of the swamp and noticed dry land: Bingo.

"Explore a wonderland in your own backyard," I murmured.

Pru turned and looked at me. "What are you muttering about?" she asked. "And why do you have that weird grin on your face?"

"No reason," I said. But the weird grin stayed there all the way to McIntire Street.

The minute we got home, I rushed upstairs and grabbed my sketch pad. I looked around until I found a good pencil to chew on. Then I hunched over my desk and tried to decide what to do about the dinosaurs.

When I looked up, it was almost dinner time, and I had filled half the pad. There was a bashful Triceratops riding the Monorail, a friendly Brontosaurus poking its head out of Elliott Bay, and a horrible Tyrannosaurus Rex climbing up the Space Needle.

But I still didn't have a plan.

Tomorrow, I decided, I would ask Nelson Richfield what the next step in our strategy should be. If he was still willing to help.

After dinner—vegetarian eggplant parmesan, which wasn't half bad, considering it was vegetarian to start with—my father leaned back in his chair and gazed around the table. "I believe," he announced, "it's time we took the Mustang out for a spin."

My father's Mustang was a vintage 1965 model and the love of his life. He'd had it for ages, and he claimed he had to drive it around Seattle every so often to keep it in mint condition. Personally, I thought it was just an excuse to show off, but I never said anything. Not having been born a twin, he probably liked the attention.

"Let's drive over to that little place by the lake and get some ice-cream cones," Sally suggested, as we assembled along the driveway for the traditional backing-out ceremony.

The garage door lifted like a curtain before the star's entrance. Then, inch by inch, the buffed turquoise flanks of the Mustang emerged. At the end of the driveway, Dad set the brake, and we all piled in.

As we started down the hill, a few drivers honked their horns, and my father smiled happily. "Those fellows know a classic when they see one," he remarked, patting the dashboard. It was something he always said when we took the Mustang out for a spin.

"Some of those fellows might be *women*, John,"

Sally observed tartly. That was something she always said too.

We circled the lake before pulling up to the ice-cream stand. It was the same stand where I used to watch Robert, and the sight of it made me uncomfortable. I wondered where he was now, whether we would even recognize each other. People could change a lot in a short time.

A car full of boys pulled in next to us. As they stared at the Mustang, my father turned to us with a smile. "Just think, girls, one of these days you'll get your licenses. And if you're very nice to the old man, he might let you borrow this heap. Believe me, the boys will start crawling out of the woodwork."

"Thank you, Daddy," Pru said stiffly. "But I don't think I'm ever going to need attention that badly."

My father looked skeptical. "The day will come," he said.

Pru groaned and scrambled out of the car, and the rest of us filed up to order cones.

A new boy was working there, digging his scoop into the frosty tubs. I ordered my favorite, maple walnut, and then stood back to watch the boys drooling over the Mustang.

I couldn't see what the fuss was about. Sometimes I wished that everyone would go back to riding horses. You never heard of people on horseback having wrecks or running out of gas. Then again, the roads probably wouldn't smell too great.

"Attention, everyone." Sally held her cone above her head like the Statue of Liberty. "I've got an important announcement to make."

My father stopped eating his ice cream. "Where," he said, "how much, and do I have to wear a tie?"

Sally laughed. Then she said, "The Golden Groat has just become a partnership."

I groaned. "Not Bev Adams, Mom! Promise me you didn't make *Bev* your partner."

"Why, no, Mattie," Sally said. "Although Bev is a perfectly nice lady who would probably make a great partner. But as a matter of fact, my new partner is our neighbor, Chloe Davis. She called yesterday to suggest it, and I accepted on the spot."

My father wiped some ice cream off his wrist. He gave my mother an unreadable look. She moved quickly into the selling phase of her announcement.

"The Davises have had a lot of business experience," she said, "and they've generously offered their time and resources to help out with the grand opening."

"Not to mention their little sidelines," my father remarked.

"Don't be cynical, John," Sally said briskly. "Lyle and Chloe have been super-supportive. Lyle's going to put our bookkeeping on his computer. And Chloe is full of ideas for the menu."

"Don't tell me," Pru sighed. "Octopus omelettes?"

"Even better," Sally said. Her eyes began to sparkle. "Why not make the Golden Groat a sort of dining cooperative? I'll bet lots of people have recipes they'd like to share with the public. So, once a week we could hold a talent show. But instead of singing or doing comedy acts, people could audition their favorite recipes."

Sally took a triumphant nibble of ice cream. "The winner would be featured as the weekly special. And any leftovers could be donated to the local food bank."

She looked around. "Well? What do you think?"

"Come to think of it," my father said, "I've had a meal or two that could qualify as a comedy act. But seriously, Sal, I like it. Diner participation. An idea whose time has come."

I liked it too, especially the part about Chloe. I could see it all — Cam and I working side by side, while Pru washed dishes in the back. "Sounds great, Mom," I said.

While Sally described her plans for the restaurant, I walked over to a picnic bench and sat down to eat my ice cream. I had just bitten into a big walnut chunk when Pru dropped down beside me.

"Speaking of the Davises," she said, "what did Cam think of your hair?"

I watched Pru lick her ice cream into a smooth dome. As the dome grew smaller and smaller, I tried to think up a snappy answer. "He thought it looked all right," I said finally. "He liked it."

"Oh, really?" Pru's ice cream looked more like a flat mesa now. "That's not what he told me. When I saw him today, he just said he was glad you got it cut, because now it would be easier to tell us apart."

My sister raised her skinny eyebrows. "Oh, I forgot to tell you. Cam invited me to a hot tub party this weekend."

After a moment, I wrapped the rest of my cone in a paper napkin. I didn't feel like eating anymore. "No kidding," I said. "A hot tub party?"

Pru watched me toss my cone in the trash. "I'm sure he meant to invite you too. It probably just slipped his mind. After all, you were pretty busy talking to your pal from the library. Nelson? Was that his name?"

But I was already trudging back to the car. I got in and stared out at the seamless surface of the lake, the dark green trees pushing out over the shore, the happy people walking beside the water.

It only reminded me of the dismal summer I had spent staring at Robert. And even though well-meaning nerds seemed to like me, it was phonies like Lydia and Pru who knew how to make the Cams and Roberts notice them. Who knew how to fit in.

As I burrowed against the Mustang's smooth white upholstery, I remembered the dinosaur project. It seemed horribly foolish now, even more foolish than the way I'd felt during the awful summer of the ice-cream boy.

And as I looked out at the lake, a tiny, terrible seed of doubt began to grow inside me. It got bigger and bigger, until finally it felt like a certainty.

Maybe, I thought as a gust of wind shattered the lake's sheen and a scrap of laughter drifted into the car, it was never going to be my year.

ten

~~~~~~

But I hadn't reckoned on Nelson.

In fact, I hadn't given Nelson a thought until I got to school and began to walk past the library. The next moment, he came bounding out the door.

"Listen," he said, "you probably thought I forgot about your project. But I've been doing some research, and I think we . . ."

I put my head down and kept walking.

"Hey, Mattie. Wait a minute."

"Sorry," I called over my shoulder. "Late for class."

"But I thought . . ." Nelson stood in the middle of the hall, staring after me. His face wore a hurt, puzzled expression.

"See you later," I called, and hurried away.

When lunchtime came, I took a seat near the windows and opened my French book. I had just found the assignment when a large book slammed down next to my lunch tray, making the milk carton jump. *Dinosaurs: An Illustrated History.*

Nelson stood over the table. "I think you owe me an explanation."

"Okay," I said quickly. "But I wasn't being rude, I just—"

He flopped down beside me. "I don't know what else you'd call it," he said.

"Look, Nelson." The kids at the next table were staring at us. I lowered my voice. "I just didn't want you to go to any more trouble. I decided not to enter that contest. So you can put your dinosaur books back where you found them."

"You *what*?" Nelson's dark eyes blazed in his thin face. "What did you say?"

"I'm not entering the contest," I said. "Do you mind?"

He shoved the hair out of his eyes with an angry swipe. "You bet I mind! And you ought to mind too. I told you we were going to win this thing, and we are. But first I want to know what happened to change your mind."

I picked up my French book. "I don't think that's any of your business. Besides, nothing happened. So I don't know where you come off acting like . . ."

Then I caught sight of Pru. She was carrying her tray to a nearby table. As I watched, Cam looked up and made room for her.

Nelson twisted around to see what I was looking at. When he turned back, his eyes weren't blazing anymore.

"I thought it might be something like that." He took a potato chip from my bag and sat crunching on it thoughtfully.

"Something like what?" I asked.

"Your sister. Dear Prudence. Your better half. Am I nuts, or is she what's behind your sudden lack of interest in the Mesozoic Era?" Nelson flicked the hair out of his eyes. "Incidentally," he said, "you're not still doing her homework assignments, are you?"

He grinned and took another chip. "Just a lucky guess. That book report last term didn't sound like her, that's all. Don't get me wrong," he added. "I'm sure she's a very nice person. But I always figured you had more on the ball. Personally, I thought it was high time you crawled out from under her thumb. So yesterday, when I saw you'd cut your hair, I figured it was time to step up and get to know you. Or try to, anyway."

He reached for another chip, but I snatched the bag away. "And then of course there's the contest. With your artistic ability and my ingenious ideas, I bet we could—"

"Nelson," I said. "Would you please shut up?"

He nodded, and looked at me expectantly.

"Thank you," I said. "The fact is, I have too much homework to spend any time on dinosaurs. So if you don't mind, I'd like to get back to my French." I picked up my book and held it firmly in front of me.

Nelson sighed. "Sorry," he said, "but as I already told you, I do mind." He lowered my book. "You seem to think I'm some kind of total stranger. But I'll bet I know you better than a lot of people do."

I glared at him. "Oh, really?"

"Yes, really. Strange as it sounds, I feel as if we've known each other for a long time. See," Nelson said eagerly, "I have this theory. Maybe the people we like were really people we knew from an earlier incarnation. Or plants we knew, if we happened to be plants. And then, when we meet them again, we're happy to see them. But not surprised, you know?"

I sighed. "Please," I said. "I don't think I can take any more reincarnation stuff."

"Why not?"

I hesitated. Then I handed Nelson the bag of potato chips. "It's a long story."

While Nelson plowed through the rest of my chips, I told him about Chloe and the channeling and Pru's Princess Mara impersonation. "And they bought it! It's just so dumb. Channeling, ESP—all that weird stuff—it doesn't exist."

Nelson raised an eyebrow. "How do you know?"

"Because I've been a twin all my life," I said, "that's how I know. Pru and I can't read each other's minds. Maybe if we could, we wouldn't drive each other up the wall."

Nelson polished off the last chip. He crumpled the bag with a loud pop. "You make being a twin sound like a fate worse than death," he remarked. "There must be some good sides to it."

He leaned forward, and I felt another theory coming on. "Maybe you guys don't have ESP," he said, "but think of all your genetic similarities. None of that messy random selection you find in most people. For instance, if you ever needed a kidney transplant, you've got the perfect donor."

Nelson grabbed one of my cookies and waved it enthusiastically. "It's incredible. You two are total replicas, right down to your tastebuds. Which means when you eat something, it must taste exactly the same to both of you." Nelson bit into the cookie and grinned. "Look on the bright side, Darwin. If you ever became a foreign dictator, you could make Pru your official taster. Nip those nasty poisoning attempts right in the bud!"

"Great, Nelson," I said. "If I ever decide to overthrow the government, I'll remember that." I grabbed my sandwich before he could eat that too. "But you're wrong. Being a twin isn't all fun and games and kidney transplants."

I took a bite of tuna and chewed on it slowly. "For instance, when I was little, I used to ask my mom which of us was real and which one was the copy. I figured that since Pru was born first, I was just the ghost-image, like something that got left in a Xerox machine by mistake."

"Wow." Nelson stared at me. He reached over and took a sip of milk. "It goes against scientific theory, but it's an amazing concept."

"That's just it," I said impatiently. "Maybe you think it would be great to have a twin, but you don't know what it's really like. You've never been called the wrong name a million times. Or had total strangers stare and point as if you'd just escaped from a circus. You don't know how it feels to be treated like a . . . a freak!"

The lunchroom was starting to clear out for the next period. I glanced over at Pru's table, but it was empty. "Anyway," I said, "that's why I got my hair cut. But it didn't do any good. Because I'm still Pru Darwin's clone, and I always will be!"

Nelson laughed. "That's why you didn't enter that contest? Clones can't win contests?" He screwed up his face in a prim expression. "We're terribly sorry, Ms. Darwin, but state law prohibits clones and their relatives from—"

"Never mind, Nelson." I gathered up my books. "You don't know what it's like to be me, and I don't know what it's like *not* to be me. So what's the use of trying to explain it?"

"Fine," Nelson said. "Give up. But you'll never find anything out if you don't try. Besides, what about me? I thought we were a team. You know, talent plus brains?" Nelson stared at me beseechingly. "Your average graffiti artist draws better than I do. I'm out three hundred dollars if you quit."

"Then find someone who can draw graffiti," I said. "The whole thing was your idea, anyway." I got up and walked out of the cafeteria.

I kept going until I reached the front steps. Then the door to the school banged and Nelson marched up behind me. "Excuse me for messing up your big exit line," he said, "but maybe I do understand. Okay, I'm not a twin. From the sound of things, that's fine with me."

Nelson's face looked pale and shiny. He gave his hair a vicious flick and peered at me. "But you're not the only person around here with feelings, Mattie Darwin. And maybe you're not the only person in the world who ever felt like a freak."

Nelson threw his books on the steps and sat next to them. "Take me, for instance," he said matter-of-factly. "I'm what you'd call your average all-around nerd. Good at math, bad at sports, and not exactly popular, despite my movie-star good looks," he added with a deprecating smile.

"My dad died when I was nine," Nelson continued, "which probably explains the sports part. Anyway, now there's just my mom and me. Not your typical nuclear family, but I don't use it as an excuse to stay mad at the world. Or to stomp around feeling sorry for myself."

"I wasn't stomping around feeling sorry for myself," I said. "And I don't think you're a nerd."

After a moment, I threw my books down too, and

sat on the steps beside Nelson. "Look," I said, "the point is, you're an only kid. You've never had to share everything—your clothes, your room, even your birthday! Everything I have, somebody else always gets to have part of it. Sometimes it drives me crazy."

The sun was directly overhead, and it made small, even shadows around us. Slowly I traced the shorn outline of my head. "I've never even had my own best friend," I said. "Pru and I have always shared her."

He glanced at me curiously. "Well, maybe your best friend shares you guys too. Ever think of that?"

"Pru and I used to have a name for her," I said. "For Heather. Back in fifth grade we called her the third twin."

Nelson squinted at me. "Heather Yamamoto? But she doesn't look like you."

I shook my head impatiently. "That's not what it means. It just means . . . " I paused. "Pru and I understood each other so well, we never had to explain things. If something was funny, we both knew it without having to say anything. If one of us was upset, we could tell automatically. And with Heather it was like that too. So we called her the third twin."

Nelson nodded slowly. "Sort of like an honor, almost?"

"Yes," I said. "I guess it was."

He gave me a sidelong glance. "Could I ever be a third twin, do you think?"

"*You?*" I almost laughed.

"I don't mean hanging out with you and your sister," he said quickly. "I mean . . . " Nelson squirmed, looking for the right word. "Friends."

We were both quiet for a moment. Then Nelson stood up and pulled me to my feet. "Maybe that's what you meant by third twin, Mattie." He grinned crookedly. "Maybe that's what you and Pru meant all along."

The bell rang right over our heads. I jumped a foot, but Nelson was already walking purposefully to the door. "I think," he said, "tomorrow we should take a look at those dinosaurs at the Science Center. If you don't mind sharing an hour with me, that is."

I studied him for a moment. "Okay," I said finally. "But if I go, will you do me a favor, Nelson?"

He grinned. "Sure. Anything."

"Would you please get your hair cut?"

He looked alarmed. "But all geniuses have long hair. Beethoven, Einstein. It's part of our image."

"Break the mold, Nelson," I said. And I headed off for French.

eleven

~~~~~~~~~~~~~~~~~~~~~~~~~~

When you've shared everything since the umbilical cord, there are times when you've got to be alone. Saturday morning was one of those times.

The minute the sun hit the bedroom window, I peeled back the covers and crept down the stairs. Early morning sunshine sparkled in the windows, and I could hear the thud of newspapers hitting the bushes as the paperboy worked his way down the block. The house felt cool and empty and full of secrets.

After a few moments of basking in solitude, I set about securing the perimeter. That was one of my dad's military phrases; it means making sure the enemy hasn't infiltrated your base of operations. In this case, it also meant making sure no one had infiltrated my cache of Frosted Flakes, hidden behind a huge sack of granola.

I settled on the rug with my cereal and turned on the TV. Saturday morning cartoons were my secret vice.

When I was a famous painter living in a loft, creating fabulous works of art, I hoped I would still have time for Frosted Flakes and cartoons. There are certain things a person should never outgrow.

Winston curled up to give himself a bath and dip a paw into my cereal bowl. I reached down to scratch him under the chin, and we both sighed contentedly.

Then the phone rang. I was about to go answer it, when I saw my mother, wearing a kerchief around her head and denim overalls, cross the hall and pick up the phone. I groaned softly. Good-bye, peace and quiet. Hello, Golden Groat Diners Cooperative.

A moment later, she stuck her head in the living room. "It's for you, Mattie. It's a boy. Its voice wobbles, anyway," she added.

Happiness clutched at my heart. Cam, I thought. It must be Cam, calling to invite me to the hot tub party.

But the minute I touched the receiver, the happy feeling shriveled up and died. "Nelson Richfield! Do you know what time it is? Mighty Mouse isn't even on yet!"

"I know what time it is," Nelson replied evenly. "Time to get moving, Darwin. The exhibit opens at ten. I suggest we meet at the front entrance. And bring some money, please. As your consultant, I am not obliged to shell out for admission fees."

"Who said anything about a consultant? I don't remember anything about a—" But he had already hung up.

I stomped into the living room, turned off the TV, and stomped out to the kitchen. Sally stood at the counter, sipping a cup of herbal tea.

She smiled at me. "You're up with the sparrows today," she remarked. "Who were you yelling at just now?"

"No one," I muttered. "Wrong number." There was no way I could explain Nelson to my mother. Not at this hour, anyway.

Then I stared at her overalls. "How long have you been up?"

She laughed. "Oh, hours and hours. Your dad's over at the restaurant, putting in some shelves. I just came back to get some of his tools. And then Chloe and I are going to pick out material for tablecloths," she added, setting down her cup. "Chloe consulted her oracles, and she said the lunar aspects point strongly toward a successful endeavor."

I took a sip of herbal tea. It tasted like something a cow would drink, if cows drank tea.

"Mom," I said, "do you really believe in crystals and lunar aspects and . . . all that stuff?" I didn't know what a lunar aspect was, but Chloe's oracles were starting to sound like the daily horoscope in the *Post-Intelligencer*.

Sally shrugged. "I guess it depends on what you want to believe, Mattie." She smiled at me. "Maybe there's something to it, and maybe there isn't. But it's kind of fun to think that stars and crystals have secret messages for us, if we look closely enough."

"Well, what about destiny?" I said. "Not the crystal ball kind. The kind where things happen for a reason. Like the way you met Dad," I added helpfully.

"Does this have something to do with that wrong number just now?" Sally asked. She was smiling at me in this terribly motherly way that made me want to leave the kitchen.

"No, of course not," I said hastily. "I just wondered, that's all. Like when you met Dad at that protest rally, did you know right then he was the man of your dreams? Or did it sort of dawn on you later?"

Sally laughed. "It wasn't a protest rally," she said. "It was pizza. I was at the student union, ordering a pizza with anchovies and pepperoni, when all of a sudden I heard this bearded fellow behind me announce that anyone who liked anchovies must be crazy. So I turned around and told him he was an old fogie, and that old fogies who didn't like anchovies had no business teaching college."

I stared at my mother in amazement. I couldn't picture her eating pizza, unless it came with a whole-wheat crust and zucchini. "Do you still like anchovies, Mom?" I asked.

Sally sighed. "I *love* anchovies," she said. "Of course, the sodium level is practically lethal, but . . ." She grinned. "It certainly got your father's attention."

"And now, years later, he's putting up shelves for your restaurant. Just think," I sighed, "it all started with pizza. You see? It had to be destiny!"

Sally pulled on her Peruvian poncho. "You might have something there, Mattie," she said. "But don't tell your dad. He still thinks it was the beard that won me over."

She went to the back door and took an appreciative sniff of morning air. "As long as you're up," she said, "why don't you come along and see the restaurant?"

"Actually," I said, "I thought I'd ride over to the Science Center this morning." I tried to sound nonchalant. "There's an exhibit I might take a look at. Animated dinosaurs."

"That sounds like fun." Sally picked up the keys to the old black Volvo and stepped outside. "Don't forget to take your sister," she called over her shoulder.

Pru was still flopped across her pillow when I crept in the room. I dug through the stuff on my desk until I found my sketch pad and was about to tiptoe out the door when Pru opened one eye. "Hey!"

"Just leaving," I said. "Catch you later."

"Wait a minute." She sat up. "I thought we were going to the mall today." She glared at me sleepily. "We *always* go to the mall on Saturday."

"Take Heather," I said. "I'm late!"

"For what? You come back here, Mattie. You never want to do anything with me anymooooore!"

I pulled on my tennis shoes and sped down the stairs, through the kitchen, and out to the garage. I was just wheeling my bike down the driveway when I glanced at the yard next door. Something was different.

It was the hot tub. It was sitting on a deck near the back porch. The wooden lid was off, and the hot water bubbled merrily, throwing clouds of steam into the cool morning air.

Then the door to the house opened, and Cam came out, wearing cut-offs and a T-shirt. He walked over to the hot tub and leaned down to test the water. Then he turned to go back inside.

I was standing there, wondering if Cam liked anchovies on his pizza, when a phrase suddenly popped into my head: "Speak now, or forever hold your peace." It was something they said in the movies when the heroine was about to marry someone she didn't love, and she stood at the altar hoping the hero would arrive in time to save her from her awful fate.

I was pretty sure they didn't say that anymore. Pru and I had been flower girls at my cousin Caroline's wedding, and as the ceremony drew to a close, I held my breath, waiting for someone to burst through the doors and proclaim that the marriage couldn't take place. By the time I started breathing again, the minister was already pronouncing them man and wife and the danger was past.

But as I stared at Cam, I suddenly understood the meaning of that phrase. It was time to speak, as my mother had spoken—not just to defend eating anchovies but to fulfill her destiny with the bearded guy in the pizza line. It was time, I realized, that Mattie Darwin took a step.

I braced myself against my bike and prayed my voice wouldn't squeak. Then I called out, "Hi!"

Cam peered over the top of the hedge. "Oh, hi," he said.

"Looks like you finally got the hot tub going," I said.

The handlebars were starting to feel slippery under my sweaty palms. Totally brilliant, Mattie, I told myself. A regular newsflash: Looks like you finally got the hot tub going. Film at 11.

Cam glanced at the hot tub. Then he looked back at me and nodded. No one said anything for a moment.

"Nice day for a bike ride," he offered finally. "They were calling for rain earlier, but it looks pretty good right now." We both peered hopefully up at the sky.

As I stood there inspecting the clouds, various humiliating speeches came to mind. "I heard you were having a party. Mind if I invite myself?" Or maybe, "You know, we just happen to have some champagne left over from New Year's. Might be the perfect thing to serve at a hot tub function." Or even, "Pru mentioned something about . . ."

No, I thought. No matter what happened, I wasn't dragging Pru into this.

But I didn't say anything. Cam and I stared up at the sky like junior forecasters. Just when I figured my neck was going to need traction, he leaned over the railing.

"Listen," he said, "we're going to try it out this afternoon. The hot tub, I mean." He paused. "My sister's invited some of her friends, so it might get a little crowded. But you're welcome to come over and check it out."

Don't let anyone tell you persistence doesn't pay off.

Slowly I relaxed my grip. The handlebars had carved red grooves in my palms, but I didn't care. I smiled casually at Cam. "Sounds like fun," I said. And then I took off down the driveway, hoping Nelson hadn't called out the National Guard.

When I got to the Science Center, Nelson was standing under the red banner, tapping his sneaker, and glaring down the street. When he saw me, a look of relief flashed across his face.

The next minute it was gone, and he was striding sternly over to the bicycle rack. "Do you know what time it is?" he said. "Where have you been?"

"I was captured by aliens from outer space. Honest. They wouldn't let me go unless I told them the Colonel's secret recipe for fried chicken."

Nelson smiled sourly. "Well, I'm sorry I had to drag you away from Mighty Mouse," he said, "but we're way behind schedule. We've only got a few days to plan, design, and build the Dino-Rama. So cartoons will have to take a backseat."

"I wasn't really watching Mighty Mouse," I said

quickly. "That's just a figure of speech." Then I stopped and stared at him. "The *what*?"

Nelson blinked impatiently. "Dino-Rama. A diorama with dinosaurs. Look, I'm not that great at art, but I've been building models since I was old enough to get an allowance. There's a store on Market Street that has all the stuff we need. Anyway, I've got the scientific know-how, and you can handle the creative side. So I figure that between us, we can do a pretty good job on a 3-D map of the Center. But with dinosaurs instead of people."

He paused uneasily. "I know, it probably sounds stupid," he said. "But—"

"Wait a second." I dug through the bike bag for my sketch pad and held it out to Nelson.

He flipped through the dinosaur sketches. Then he studied them again, and a slow grin spread across his face. "See?" he said. "Great minds think alike."

I stuck the pad in my backpack, and we walked through the Science Center toward the admission booth. While we waited in line, I peered over at Nelson. He looked different, I thought. Better, for some reason.

Then I laughed. "Nelson, you got a haircut!"

"I said I would, didn't I?" Nelson gave his head a defensive toss, but there wasn't any hair left to toss. He ended up scratching his nose instead.

"It looks very nice," I assured him. "You'll see, you can be just as big a genius with short hair."

"Who said anything about geniuses?" Nelson handed the girl at the window six dollars. "Come on," he said, grabbing the tickets. "You make the sketches, I'll take notes."

I was still holding out my admission money. Without a word, I put the three dollars in my pocket and followed Nelson up the steps to the exhibit.

For the next hour, we studied the life-sized replicas of Stegosaurus and Tyrannosaurus Rex. Computerized machinery made the models lift their heads and roar until eerie, thundering cries filled the hall. Smaller displays showed the earth as it had once looked, along with cases of dinosaur footprints and fossilized eggs. While Nelson took notes, I stared at the giant lizards and filled up my pad with drawings.

At the final display, Nelson studied my sketches. "Nice work," he said. "Very nice. I'm impressed."

He leaned against the guard rail. "Now, about the dinos. Even though I'm partial to the more obscure guys, like Saltopus and Lambeosaur, we're probably better off sticking with the celebrities. The Bronto, the Rex—the ones everyone knows."

"And Pterodactyls," I put in, "flying over downtown Seattle!"

"Don't forget, it's a diorama," Nelson warned me. "If we want stuff flying around, we'll have to rig it up. Besides," he added, "technically speaking, the flying reptiles weren't dinosaurs."

"But they are crowd pleasers," I pointed out.

"We'll think about it." Nelson checked his watch. "Right now, I'd better catch the bus over to the model shop and see what they have in the way of prehistoric vegetation."

We were standing next to the giant Stegosaurus. It suddenly lifted its pointed head and let out a piercing cry.

"What about the dinosaurs?" I asked. "Can we buy models of them too?"

Nelson shook his head. "I haven't figured out the scale, but I think the store-bought dinos will be the wrong size. So," he said, "you'll have to make them."

"*Me*? But I thought you . . ."

Nelson sighed. "Look, Darwin, this was supposed to be your project, remember? Besides, anyone who can draw—and I think we've established you draw rather well—can mold a decent dinosaur. Don't worry, I'll show you how."

He stuck the notebook in his back pocket. Then he glanced at me curiously. "Did you ever realize what an interesting name you have? Darwin, I mean. He was the guy who came up with the theory of evolution."

We walked past the cases of dinosaur bones toward the exit. "Yes, I know," I said. "My dad claims we're related. Uncle Charlie, he calls him."

Nelson laughed. Then he zipped up his jacket. "Well, I'd better get going."

I tried to give him my admission money, but he

frowned it away. "This part's on me. When we get to the papier mâché, I'll bill you, okay?"

"Or you can deduct it from the prize money," I suggested.

Nelson smiled. "That's the idea, Darwin. Positive thinking."

We reached the steps of the pavilion. The sky had softened to a deep azure blue and, for a moment, I felt as if Nelson and I were tiny figures in a giant diorama of sky, white arches, and miniature buildings. "When do we start work on the Dino-Rama?" I asked.

Nelson paused. "I should have everything ready by tomorrow. And don't worry about my mother. She's used to me messing up the kitchen with my works of genius."

He started toward the gate. "See you tomorrow, Mattie," he called. "And if the Prune gives you any trouble, you tell her evolution doesn't happen overnight." He paused. "Just ask Uncle Charlie. Or Tyrannosaurus Rex, for that matter."

"What's that supposed to mean?"

Nelson smiled crookedly. "Nothing terrible," he said. "Hey, there's my bus. Gotta go!"

I watched him take off down the street in long, loping strides. Just when I decided that Nelson was the weirdest person I'd ever met, he said or did something to make me change my mind. Maybe that meant I was just as weird as he was. Or that Nelson really did know me better than a lot of people did. Or maybe we were reincarnated fern fronds from the same prehistoric jungle.

Whatever the reason, it didn't make Nelson any easier to figure out. At any rate, he'd gotten a haircut. So at least he was a little easier to look at.

I looked at my watch. It was almost noon. Hoisting my backpack, I hurried down the steps, the roars of the dinosaurs still echoing in my ears.

And then, as I started to unlock my bike, I wondered what on earth a person wore to a hot tub party.

twelve

~~~~~~~~~~~~~~~~~~~~~~~~~~~~~~~~~

When I got home, I went to the closet and stared at my clothes. Blouses and skirts, jeans and sweatshirts stared back. None of them looked like appropriate hot tub attire.

I was just about to check under the bed for further fashion options when I noticed my ancient red-and-white bathing suit crumpled on the closet floor. I hated that bathing suit—it made me look like the world's flattest barber pole. For once I wished that the noted fashion expert Prunehilda were here to advise me.

But she wasn't. The horrible barber pole suit would just have to do.

The sound of the phone ringing cut through the house. Grabbing the bathing suit, I ran to my parents' room and picked up the receiver.

"Do you still want to go to the mall?" Heather asked. "I finished my practicing, so my mom said—"

Poor Heather, I thought, no Mighty Mouse for her. "This isn't Pru, sushi brains. It's me, Mattie."

"Mattie!" she said. "Where have you been? Pru said you took off and wouldn't tell her where you were going."

I stretched out on the king-size bed and wrapped the phone cord around my hand. "I'll tell you later," I said. "But first, we're invited to a party next door. The Davises have hooked up their hot tub."

There was a long pause. "I don't know, Mattie," Heather said doubtfully. "I don't know anything about hot tubs." She lowered her voice. "What if they make us take our clothes off? What about germs?"

I sighed. "Heather, if the neighbors were running a nudist colony, I think we'd have noticed by now. And I'm sure the water is too hot to grow germs. Look," I said, "think of this as a culturally enriching experience. Pretend you're an anthropologist observing a primitive tribe. Besides," I added, "you'll finally get to meet the great Cam."

"Oh," Heather said, "I already know Cam. He's in my honors Latin class."

I sat up. "He is? Cam? *Our* Cam?"

"Yeah, he had to take tons of it back at his old school. He says the stuff we translate is easy compared with what he used to get."

"Oh," I said.

Then I heard the front door open and the sound of my father's heavy footsteps cross the hall. I scrambled off the bed. "Meet me in ten minutes," I told Heather. "And bring your bathing suit."

Pru must have taken the bus to the mall, I thought. Considering how often the buses ran, it would be hours before she got back. Things were working out perfectly.

I pulled on my barber pole suit, threw on some jeans, and dashed downstairs. My father was in the kitchen, fixing himself a baloney sandwich from his private supply of nitrate-loaded lunchmeat.

"Hi," I said. "How's the Moldy Oat coming? When do we get to see it?"

"It's almost finished," he sighed, "and so am I. I spent all morning putting up shelves and painting woodwork and ordering food for the grand opening. Which is"—he checked the calendar on his watch—"approximately fifty hours from now."

He leaned on the counter and took big, tired bites of his sandwich. "Did you know," he said between bites, "that there are businesses that do nothing but supply restaurants with bean sprouts?"

My father shook his head. "How did I get talked into this, Mattie? I'm a history professor. I never even *minored* in carpentry, let alone spent a whole morning ordering bean sprouts."

I shrugged. "Hurricane Sally," I told him. "Whoosh."

He nodded. "That reminds me. Your mother has gone to pick out tablecloths with Cleopatra."

"Chloe," I said.

"Whatever." He straightened with a groan and went to the refrigerator and took out a can of beer. "If you need anything," he said, "I'll be in my study, working on a piece for the *History Quarterly*."

I watched him pick up his sandwich and beer and hobble out of the kitchen. Poor Dad. If only he'd kept his mouth shut about the anchovies, his life might have been completely different. Sometimes destiny could play cruel tricks, I thought, as I ran outside to wait for Heather.

At precisely 12:36, a big white Cadillac drove slowly down the street and pulled up in front of our house. A moment later, Pru hopped out, followed by someone with short blond hair and long tan legs. Someone, in fact, a lot like Lydia Carthage.

I watched them gather up their shopping bags. This was my own fault, I told myself. I'd left Pru to her own devices, and now I'd have to pay the price.

Sure enough, she was walking across the lawn with a big smile on her face. "Guess who I ran into at the mall?" she said.

I stared at Lydia. "I can't imagine."

"Remember that party over at Cam's? I told Lydia it was okay if she came too."

Lydia was nodding so hard that her hair bounced. "Yes, Pru told me it was okay. I think hot tubs are so relaxing, don't you?"

I had a pretty good idea why Lydia thought they were so relaxing, but I didn't say anything. I watched Pru bundle up her shopping bags and lead Lydia around the side of the house.

As they passed the garage, Lydia stopped. "Wow," she said, "is that yours?" She was gazing at the Mustang's turquoise hood.

"It's our dad's," Pru admitted.

"But it's great!" Lydia said, walking around to get a better look. "It's so . . . sixties!"

"So's our dad," I told her.

Lydia laughed. "Gee, I wish we had a car like that. My father always trades ours in on the latest model." Then she glanced at Pru. "Hey, do you know where the keys are? Let's take it for a ride!"

I stared at Lydia. "Are you nuts or something? We can't drive. Even if we could, we'd never steal Dad's Mustang. He'd kill us!"

Lydia looked annoyed. "I didn't mean we'd take it to Las Vegas," she said. "Just, you know, up and down the block. But if you don't want to, forget I said anything."

Pru shot me a murderous glance. "Come on, Lydia," she said. "Let's go change."

Clutching their bags, they disappeared up the back stairs, and I sat down on the porch to wait for Heather.

Five minutes later, a strange creature appeared at the foot of the driveway. The creature's nose was plastered with zinc oxide. On its head was a pink rubber bathing cap; flesh-colored noseplugs hung around its neck. Under one arm, the creature carried a large inflatable duck.

As I started down the steps, the creature hung its head, and the plastic flower on the pink bathing cap drooped pathetically.

"Heather," I said, when I reached the driveway, "we are *not* going to the beach. We are *not* going to the swimming pool. We are going to a hot tub party!"

"I know," Heather said miserably. "But I couldn't tell my mom that. She wouldn't have let me come if she knew it was a . . . a . . ."

I sighed. "It's not an orgy, Heather. It's just a big tub of hot water. Now give me that stupid duck, and let's get over there before . . ."

But it was too late. The screen door slammed behind me. I turned around, and I practically had a heart attack.

Pru and Lydia stood on the porch. At least I thought it was Pru. Her hair was teased within an inch of its life; it stood out from her head in a bizarre reddish-brown cloud. She was wearing an extremely small, extremely pink bathing suit, and enough makeup to make Bev Adams sick with envy. Or maybe just plain sick.

Lydia had gone for a different look—namely, the junior temptress look. I didn't know what would happen when her black leather bikini touched hot water, but I could see enough of Lydia to get a pretty good idea.

I looked down at my barber pole suit and then at Heather, who was still clutching her duck. As we huddled together in the driveway, the temptresses strolled past us, crossed the lawn, and disappeared around the hedge.

"Was that really Pru?" Heather asked.

"Give or take a few decades." I yanked the cap off her head and wiped the zinc oxide off her nose. "Leave your rubber ducky on the porch," I ordered. "It's time to secure the perimeter."

"What are you talking about, Mattie?" Heather said. But she set the duck on the front steps and faced me obediently.

I stood in the driveway like Field Marshall Darwin, surveying my terrain. "I'm talking about enemy infiltration, Heather. Divide and conquer. It's the oldest trick in the book."

I peered through the hedge at the Davises' backyard, where the chatter of voices could be heard. "Heather," I said, "all's fair in love and war. Right?"

Heather rubbed her nose. "I guess so."

"In that case," I said, "I don't think Pru will mind if we stage a small counteroffensive." I tugged at the straps of my bathing suit. "Remember," I said, "whatever happens, stay calm. And now—forward march!"

But when we reached the hot tub, Pru and Lydia

were nowhere in sight. Zee Davis's head and shoulders popped out of the bubbling water. Five other heads rose above the rim of the tub. Judging by their long stringy hair and jutting shoulder blades, the heads belonged to five scrawny teenage boys.

"We'll be out in a sec," Zee called. "This is my band, the Paramedics. They're not really paramedics," she explained. "We just liked the name."

One of the Paramedics raised a damp hand. "Nice hair," he said. He was pointing at me. "Where did you get it cut?"

"The Animal Cage," I told him.

He nodded enthusiastically. "My cousin works there. Big blond guy? Goes by the name of Ramon?"

I thought about holding his head underwater, just to teach him never to mention his cousin again. But I didn't want to tangle with the other Paramedics. They might be stronger than they looked.

"The band's been practicing all week," Zee told us. "We're going to perform at the opening of the Gilded Grotto."

"The Golden Groat?" I said.

Zee shrugged and nodded. "Time's up," she said to the Paramedics. Then she climbed out of the tub and stood dripping on the deck. "Come on," she added. "Let's go find Cam."

Cam was in the kitchen, filling glasses with ice. Pru and Lydia sat at the kitchen table, beaming at him. They stopped beaming when they saw us. "Oh, hi,"

Cam said. "I was just getting the girls here some kiwi coolers. Want one?"

Zee shook her head. "You can take your harem out to the tub now, Cameroon," she said. "We're going upstairs to practice."

The Paramedics looked like they'd rather stay and talk to Lydia and Pru, but Zee herded them out of the kitchen. A few moments later we heard a muffled drum beat, followed by weird, unearthly yodeling.

Cam winced. "That's Zee," he explained. "Singing."

I glanced at Heather. "Maybe she should try opera."

He sighed. "It's probably better not to encourage her." He put the kiwi coolers on a tray. "Come on," he said. "Let's go try out the hot tub."

When we got out to the deck, I peered into the tub. Now that the moment had arrived, the tub looked much bigger and deeper than it had from our driveway. As I stared down at the foaming water, I wondered what would happen if you poured in a few gallons of bubble bath. McIntire Street would probably be buried for months.

Under the water, a long bench ran all the way around the tub. I watched Cam climb in and sit down. Then the rest of us got in the tub. Pru and Lydia sat on one side of Cam, and Heather and I sat on the other.

A rush of hot water swirled against my legs. A cool breeze stole across the deck, ruffling my hair. It made the heat of the water feel even more intense. Then a stronger jet of water began to massage my skin, and I sank down, enjoying the bubbling warmth. Lydia was right, I thought. This was pretty relaxing. I leaned my head against the rim of the tub and closed my eyes.

All of a sudden I heard Lydia's loud squeaky voice. "I heard you're working on a project for the art contest," she was saying. "I'd love to see it sometime."

I opened my eyes to see Lydia batting her eyelashes at Cam. I'd never seen anyone actually do this before, and I thought it made Lydia look incredibly stupid.

Cam took a sip of his cooler. "I'd show it to you," he said, "but I already turned it in." He grinned. "The way I figure it, if they've got to give someone three hundred dollars, it might as well be me."

Pru turned to him with a bright smile. "Mattie's working on a project too. Something about dinosaurs crawling up the Space Needle, I think."

I stared at Pru. "How do you know about that?" I said, and then it dawned on me. My sketch pad! Pru must have gone through my desk and found my drawings.

She smiled innocently. "You *told* me all about it, Mattie. Don't you remember? How you and that library kid were working on this dinosaur thing together?"

"What library kid?" Lydia asked. Then she gave a startled laugh. "Oh, no. Not that geeky kid with the long hair. You're not working on an art project with *him*?"

I glared at Pru. "I didn't tell you anything. You were snooping through my stuff!"

"Hey, maybe it was twin ESP," Cam said. He looked pleased at the idea. "Maybe you guys accidentally read each other's minds."

"Maybe," Pru said, but I could tell she wasn't done yet. "Actually," she continued, "Mattie has lots of weird projects."

"Pru—"

"She reads library books aloud in an English accent. She's been doing it all summer," Pru said triumphantly. "She sounds just like Alfred Hitchcock."

"I do not," I said, but it was too late. Cam was looking around as if he expected to see Alfred pop out of the water any second.

I cleared my throat and looked at Pru. Okay, I thought. Let the Games begin.

"At least," I said loudly, "I don't hide in the bushes and spy on people. And I don't steal Dad's razor and hack my legs to pieces, even though we're not supposed to shave them yet. And at least," I announced, as a shocked silence settled over the tub, "I don't write 'Mrs. Cameron Davis' all over the cover of my notebook!"

The afternoon was growing cooler, and a haze of steam rose from the water. I felt Heather nudge me with her foot and heard her say, "Mattie!" But I was busy staring through the steam at Pru. For a moment I didn't notice how red her face was getting. All I could see was her mouth opening and shutting, like a giant carp gasping for air.

Her eyelids quivered, and her head fell forward.

Lydia looked startled. "What's the matter? Is she having a seizure or something? I read where you're supposed to put an eraser in people's mouths when they're having a seizure. In case they try to swallow their tongue."

I studied Pru. She wasn't having a seizure, unless you counted Princess Mara's timely arrival. "It's okay," I told Lydia. "She's just channeling."

But Cam was looking at Pru too. "No," he said. "I don't think she is." And with that, he scooped Pru out of the water and carried her into the house.

"I've seen this happen before," Cam assured us as he put Pru down on the couch and settled her with her head between her knees. "That hot water's just too much for some people. Makes 'em drop like flies. Don't worry, though," he added. "I'm sure she'll be okay."

I wanted to tell him that Pru hadn't written "Mrs. Cameron Davis" all over her notebook—just in one corner, really. I wanted to point out that my father didn't own a razor. But Cam and Heather were too busy hovering over Pru to listen. Lydia was saying that when people fainted, you were supposed to wave ammonia under their nose, so Cam trotted out to the kitchen and came back with a bottle of Windex.

I sat beside Pru and rubbed her shriveled hands. Right at the moment, she really did look like a great big wrinkled-up prune. Just as Lydia leaned forward and prepared to brandish the Windex, Pru came to.

"What's that for?" she said, looking grumpy. "And what are you guys standing around *staring* at?" It was time to go home.

Heather and I guided Pru across the lawn and up the stairs to bed. We left her propped up on a mountain of pillows, clutching a washcloth and reading a magazine. We had just settled on the front steps to dry off, when my father came out on the porch and yawned. He always looked sleepy after he'd been working on one of his articles.

"What's wrong with Prune?" he remarked. "She asked me to get her a glass of ginger ale. You kids never want ginger ale unless you're sick."

Fortunately I didn't have to answer because the Volvo pulled into the driveway, and my mother and Chloe got out. They were both carrying bundles from Sur La Table, a very expensive kitchen store at the Pike Place Market.

My father looked at the bags, and his jaws clenched briefly. I knew he was going to say something about people who bought tablecloths at Sur La Table when they could get very nice ones at Woolworth's for half the price.

My mother knew it too. "They were on sale," she said defensively. "The tag says they're recommended by Julia Child."

My father snorted sarcastically. "In that case," he began, "by all *means* —"

As usual, he didn't get a chance to finish. Just as my mother clamped her lips shut, Chloe spotted Heather and me sitting on the steps drying our wet hair. "Did you kids go swimming?"

"Actually," I said, "we just tried out your hot tub."

Chloe beamed. "Isn't it fantastic?" Then she stopped beaming. "I hope Cam warned you guys not to stay in too long," she said sternly. "People can actually faint if they're not used to the hot water."

I nodded. "Yes," I said, "I've heard that too."

My mother started past us up the steps. "Oh, by the way," she said, "we stopped at your mother's import shop, Heather. I never realized it was right in the Public Market. Anyway, I'm glad we bumped into her, because she promised to make some authentic sushi for the grand opening of the Golden Groat."

Heather glanced at me. I could tell she was trying to picture her mother serving up sushi in her nice red suit while the Paramedics howled in the background. I was trying to picture it too. I took a deep breath. "Mom," I said. "About the band."

My father looked startled. "The band?"

Sally was busy juggling her parcels. "Oh, yes, the band. That was Chloe's idea. I think live music will add a very distinctive touch, don't you?" She looked around brightly. No one said a word.

After Heather had gone home, I sat on the steps staring at the yard next door and wondering why every time I tried to impress Cam Davis, I ended up looking like a jerk.

Maybe there were secret rules that determined a person's destiny but nobody told you what they were. They probably had something to do with my mother's karma theory. There was a movie theater owner who wouldn't give senior citizen discounts, and Sally always said his karma and seventy-five cents wouldn't get him on the uptown bus.

Well, I thought, whatever those secret rules were, I'd sure like to get my hands on them. Because right now, all I had going for me was Nelson and the Dino-Rama.

And karmically speaking, that didn't seem like a whole lot to work with.

thirteen

~~~~~~

Somehow I'd figured that Nelson would live in a big gloomy mansion with dusty windowsills and shabby furniture. A creaky old house full of shadows and odd corners, with a bubbling beaker here and there.

In other words, a mad scientist's house.

Instead, when Mrs. Richfield pulled into the driveway on Sunday, all I saw was a small yellow ranch house with a neatly mowed lawn and a carport instead of a garage.

Nelson's mom hadn't been what I'd pictured either. She was a lot younger than I'd expected, with short brown hair and a calm, warm smile. But her dark eyes were just like Nelson's, sharp and alert.

"Why don't you two get to work in the kitchen?" she said. "I've covered the table with newspaper, so you can be as messy as you want."

"Thanks, Mom," Nelson said. "Let me get the diorama," he told me, "and then we'll cook up some dinosaur dough."

"I'll help you," I said quickly, and I followed him down the hall.

Nelson's room looked like an accumulation of everything that was inside Nelson's head. Books were crammed into every square inch of space. The walls were filled with weird maps and lists. Next to the unmade bed, a chess board was set up on a cluttered card table.

I stared at a chart that was thumb-tacked to the wall. "What are those numbers for?"

"Postal chess," Nelson answered. He was struggling to lift an object covered with canvas. "I have ten games going at the moment. You write down a move and send it to a player in New York or Wichita or Maine. Then the other person has a certain amount of time to decide on his move and send it back."

"Don't you forget which game is which?"

Nelson sighed. "That's what those numbers are for," he said. "Here, grab that end."

As I picked up the Dino-Rama, I peeked under the canvas, and I almost dropped the whole thing on Nelson's foot. There, painstakingly painted and arranged, was a complete replica of the Center, right down to a teeny elevator hugging the side of the Space Needle.

"Nelson," I said, "what do we need dinosaurs for? It's . . . perfect!"

"It's not perfect by a long shot," Nelson said. "I didn't start painting until last night, so it's pretty sloppy in places. And you're wrong about the dinosaurs. Every kid who ever built a Messerschmitt is going to turn in a model like this. The dinosaurs are what will set it apart. Besides," he added, "the Science Center won't be able to resist a plug for their exhibit. We can't miss!"

"Well, okay," I said. "I'd just hate to mess up your beautiful model, that's all."

"Don't worry about it," he said. "Now, come on. We've got work to do."

While Nelson mixed the salt dough, I took out my sketch pad and arranged my drawings on the table. As soon as the dough was ready, Nelson handed me a pin cushion and a box of toothpicks. "You're all set," he said. "You make the dinos while I fix the paint job." With a friendly pat on the back, he cleared a space at the table and we set to work.

The first dinosaur came out looking more like a pre-historic blob. I wadded it up and tried again. This time it looked like an unbaked muffin.

I tossed the dough back in the pan. "Nelson," I said, "this is useless. The only stuff I ever made out of dough were doughnuts, and they weighed about three pounds apiece."

"It'll get easier once the dough hardens a little," Nelson said calmly. "Just keep studying the pictures."

I stared at my sketch of Triceratops. Then I rolled a ball of fresh dough between my fingers and began to make some horns on it with my toothpick. "So," I said, "what did your father do? Before he died, I mean."

The minute I said it, I wanted to stuff my mouth with dinosaur dough. But Nelson didn't look offended. He paused, his paintbrush poised over the miniature Opera House. "My father," he said proudly, "was an inventor. And I'm going to be one too."

"No kidding." I gave my dinosaur a squat body and a beaky face. "What did he invent?"

"A whole bunch of stuff. A car that runs on water. Solar-powered lightbulbs. Self-shining shoes. He had nearly a hundred patents pending when he got multiple sclerosis. That's this disease of the nervous system," Nelson explained, "and it affected his coordination. So it got hard for him to do much inventing after a while." He sounded very matter-of-fact about it, as if he were explaining how a toaster works.

"So how come your mom never remarried?" I said, trying to sound matter-of-fact too. My dinosaur was starting to look almost recognizable. I took a pin from the cushion and gave him a little smile. "I mean, she isn't too old to get married again. And she's certainly pretty enough."

Nelson gazed at me sternly. "Some people," he said, "only fall in love with one person their entire life. I happen to think my mother is one of those people. And I probably am too."

"Well, I hope I'm not." I reached in the pan for more dough. "I hope I'll fall in love with all kinds of people and have lots of interesting experiences. Before I eventually settle down, of course."

A pinched-lipped expression had crept over Nelson's face. "That sounds very irresponsible," he said.

"Good grief, Nelson! People don't fall in love because it's *responsible*. You make romance sound about as exciting as . . . as choosing from the four major food groups or something!"

Nelson sighed. He put down his paintbrush. "In that case," he said, "there's probably no point in telling you that I like you, Mattie Darwin. That I happen to be a rather major fan of yours, in fact. But I guess I'm just not the type of guy who's going to sweep a person off her feet. So I might as well learn to live with it." With a philosophic shrug, Nelson turned back to his painting.

As the dough hardened between my fingers, I tried to figure out what had happened during the last thirty seconds. When I couldn't, I looked at Nelson. He was bent over the Dino-Rama, doing a little trim work with the tip of his brush.

"Nelson?" I said. "What on earth are you talking about?"

He looked up calmly. "I was declaring my feelings for you, Mattie. Which probably sounds pretty weird, given the fact that we're only eighth graders and probably not qualified to be discussing love in the first place."

"Oh," I said. I was starting to catch on. Nelson Richfield had a crush on me.

I waited to feel something—horror, embarrassment,

outrage. No one had ever had a crush on me before. It had always been the other way around. This was a whole new experience.

After a few moments, I decided I didn't mind. After all, major fans weren't that easy to come by. And it might be good practice for the next time someone had a crush on me.

I wondered if Cam went around declaring his feelings for people. Somehow I didn't think so, but it couldn't hurt to be prepared.

"Well, thank you, Nelson," I said finally. "You certainly have a unique way of expressing things."

He looked pleased. "Really? You think so?"

"Absolutely," I said. "But in the future, you should try not to sound so analytical. It makes a person feel like she's been stuck under a microscope or something."

"But I can't help that," Nelson said. "I *am* analytical."

I sighed. "Never mind. I guess you'll just have to find out the hard way."

Nelson nodded. He looked almost cheerful about it. "Probably," he agreed. "Sort of like the scientific method. Trial and error."

He picked up his paintbrush again. "Anyway, Mattie, I appreciate your honesty. You're the first girl I ever declared my feelings for, and I was kind of wondering how it would go." Nelson's shoulders hunched up and his nose gave a twitch. "I think it went pretty well, don't you?"

Three hours later, Mrs. Richfield peeked into the room. "How's it going?" she asked. "I was just wondering if Mattie would like to stay for dinner. As soon as the Dino-Rama's ready, that is."

Nelson beamed. "Take a look," he said. "I told you she was a real artist."

Mrs. Richfield bent over to peer at the Dino-Rama. Then she smiled. "It's wonderful!" she exclaimed. "Really, Mattie. Those dinosaurs are absolutely irresistible."

I blushed. "Nelson did most of the work."

"Baloney," he said. "You can get nearly all that stuff out of a kit. But not this little guy." He gazed fondly at the Triceratops, who was lined up for a ride on the Monorail, an eager smile on his reptilian face.

"I get off work early tomorrow," Mrs. Richfield said. "I can bring the Dino-Rama over to school then. Now," she went on, "why don't you call your mother and tell her you'll be joining us for dinner? It's just tuna casserole, but Nelson's always liked it."

"Does it have real tuna in it?" I asked quickly. "Not abalone? Or octopus? Or tuna-textured tofu?"

Mrs. Richfield looked startled. "Why, no," she said. "It's just plain old tuna and noodles."

Plain old tuna and noodles, I thought, might possibly be the five best words in the English language.

I smiled at Mrs. Richfield. "Food allergy," I explained. "Just had to make sure. So," I asked, "where's the phone? I'm starving!"

After dinner, Nelson and I packed the Dino-Rama in an earthquake-proof crate, and then Mrs. Richfield drove me home. As I was getting out of the station wagon, the big white Cadillac pulled up across the street, and Pru jumped out.

I turned and waved at Mrs. Richfield, and Pru turned and waved at Lydia, who was sitting in front with her father, the airline pilot. Then the cars drove off in opposite directions.

Pru picked up her shopping bags and started toward the house. "Hi, Pru," I called. "If you thought you were invisible, you're wrong." I paused. "Where have you been?"

Pru blinked. "What do you care, Twinkie?"

"I just wondered, that's all. And don't call me Twinkie."

Carefully Pru examined a grease spot in the driveway. "I went shopping," she said. "With Lydia."

"I thought you guys went shopping yesterday."

Pru picked up her Wyndham's bag. "I can go shopping if I want to. What's the big deal? After all," she said, "you're too busy hanging around with that awful geek to do anything fun anymore."

"Nelson isn't a geek," I said. "Anyway, he got a haircut. He looks a lot better —"

"He is so a geek," Pru said calmly. "And you know what? I think you're turning into one too."

"I am not!"

"Yes, you are." Pru started to walk toward the house. "Well, that's fine with me," she said over her shoulder. "I've got my own friends. So you can hang out with all the weirdos you want, Mattie Darwin. It doesn't bother me one bit."

"Good," I yelled. "I will—*Prunehilda*!"

One of the MacGruder kids from down the block was riding past on his bike. He dug his sneaker into the curb and stopped to watch the fight.

Pru had just opened her mouth to answer when she was interrupted by a clash of cymbals, followed by a loud shriek.

We both peered up at the Davis house, where another Paramedics rehearsal was just getting underway. Then we turned and glared at Stevie MacGruder, who scrambled back on his bike and sped off down the street.

I started toward the steps, but Pru beat me to the door. "Geek," she muttered as she brushed past.

"Creep."

"Twink!"

"Dried-up prune!"

"Weirdo!" Pru shouted. "Weirdo, weirdo, weird—"

Sally came marching out of the kitchen. "I've heard just about enough," she said. "Now what's going on out here?"

Pru didn't answer. Instead, she picked up her bags and marched up the stairs. At the landing, she turned and mouthed the word "Twink" before banging into the bedroom and slamming the door.

Sighing, I followed my mother out to the kitchen. The room was warm with the smell of baking. "Pru and I were having a slight difference of opinion," I told her.

Sally studied me. "So I noticed. Well, did you have a good time at . . . what was their name again?"

"The Richfields," I said. Sally was wearing that horrible motherly expression, and it made me feel nervous. "Pru says I'm turning into a geek," I said, to change the subject. "But she's the one who's turning into something—a big phony snob, that's what. Not that it surprises me," I added. "She's been going downhill for a while."

"That's funny," Sally said with a half smile. "She says the same thing about you."

A pie sat cooling on the counter. I went over and took a sniff. Rhubarb. Not my favorite, which is pecan covered with whipped cream and is available only at non-health-food restaurants, but I had to admit it smelled pretty good.

I broke off a piece of crust and sat down at the counter. "Mom?" I asked. "Were you upset when you found out you were going to have twins? Or were you glad?"

Sally cut a large piece of pie. Then she set it on a plate

in front of me. "Upset? I was terrified. And thrilled, of course." She handed me a fork. "But you know, you were always such different kids. Pru was very fussy, but you were such a sunny baby. I'd give you your favorite toy, and you'd lie there for hours, chewing on it and drooling happily away."

"Really?" I said. I loved the thought of being a sunny baby. "What was my favorite toy?"

Sally frowned. "It was purple, and it had a long neck. A giraffe? No, not a giraffe. Wait," she said, "I know. It was one of those Flintstone characters."

"The *Flintstones*? You mean you let me sit around chewing on Barney Rubble, Mom? Yuck!"

"Not Barney Rubble." Sally smiled. "Now I remember. It was Dino. Their pet dinosaur."

"Pet dinosaur?" Oh no, I thought. Wait until Nelson heard this one. "Believe it or not, Mom," I began, "there's this project I'm working on, and it's . . ."

Then I stopped and concentrated on my rhubarb pie. I probably shouldn't say anything until we won.

"A project?" Sally looked interested.

"It's not really a project," I said quickly. "More like a homework assignment. Anyway, you were talking about how Pru and I were so different," I reminded her. "So how come we can't get along the way you and Dad do? I mean, Dad likes to read war books, and you go on peace marches. You play the Grateful Dead and he listens to Frank Sinatra. He pretends to work on those history articles and we both know he's in there taking a nap. But you never say a word."

Sally covered the pie with a cloth. "It's partly age," she said. "It took me a long time to figure out your dad was never going to be exactly like me. He has his weirdnesses, and I have mine. But as long as we respect each other and love each other, the other stuff doesn't seem that important."

"Why can't Pru respect my weirdnesses?"

Sally sat down at the counter and frowned thoughtfully. "I think," she said, "it's probably because you were born in Gemini, the sign of the Twins — an astrological double whammy. I should have planned things so that you would be born under Libra, the sign of the Scale. That's a very balanced sign. It would have been perfect for twins."

"Wow, Mom," I said, "that's really deep. Maybe you should write an astrology column for *People* magazine or something."

"All right, Mattie," she said. "Then let me put it another way. You're both teenagers, and things will probably get worse before they get better. But when you're old and married, believe me, you'll remember the joys of having someone with the same sense of humor and the same temperament and the same habits —"

"And the same taste in men," I added. "But it doesn't matter, because we'll probably never get married, since no one can tell us apart. I mean, how can you propose to someone if you don't know who you're proposing to?"

Sally picked up some of my pie crust and popped it in her mouth. "I don't remember that wrong number asking to speak to Pru," she said. She gave me a meaningful glance.

I groaned. "That was Nelson. And I would never ever marry Nelson, even if he can tell us apart. Nelson is very unathletic. I doubt if Nelson has ever seen a tennis racquet in his whole life."

My mother looked puzzled. "What does tennis have to do with all this?"

"Nothing," I said quickly. I picked up my fork and took a bite of pie. Then I took another bite. "Hey, this is great. You should definitely serve it next weekend. At the grand opening."

Sally gave me a long, cold look. "Mattie," she said, "in case it slipped your mind, the grand opening of the Golden Groat is tomorrow night."

I stopped eating. "Tomorrow night? Who ever heard of a restaurant opening on a week night, Mom?"

Sally paused. "For your information, Mattie, Chloe picked the date on the basis of sound astrological practices. The moon will just be entering Leo, which is the perfect sign for new endeavors."

"Wonderful, Mom," I mumbled. "I just hope the food critics at the *Seattle Post-Intelligencer* get assigned on the basis of sound astrological practices. I mean, wouldn't you hate it if no one showed up?"

My mother fixed me with a warning glance. "Don't worry, we'll get plenty of coverage in the *Queen Anne Gazette*. At any rate, the doors open at five for the dinner seating, so I'd like you and Pru to come over right after school and help get things ready. And once the doors are open, you will both be on your best behavior, if I have to brainwash you and tie you to a lamppost!"

I pictured what it would be like to spend a whole evening tied to a lamppost with Prunehilda. It was an extremely gruesome thought.

Quickly I took another bite of rhubarb. "Really, Mom," I said, pointing at the plate. "Great pie."

I just hoped someone besides me would show up to eat it.

fourteen

"Four o'clock," Nelson announced. He set the Dino-Rama on the art teacher's desk. "Made the deadline with seconds to spare."

Mr. Gruenfeld was in the back, unloading supplies. When he heard our voices, he came out to look at the Dino-Rama.

"Well, now," he said. "Looks like you folks have got something here."

"We know that," Nelson said briskly. "So when do they announce the winners?"

Mr. Gruenfeld studied the Dino-Rama. He scratched his head. "Yep," he said, "that's a fine piece of work. But I have to warn you, the competition for this thing is pretty tough."

"We're not worried," Nelson said firmly. "When do we find out?"

"The sponsors will announce the prizes by Friday. If the winner is from Puget Sound Academy, we'll hold an assembly."

"Fine," Nelson said. "We'll be there."

While they were admiring the Dino-Rama, I walked over to look at the other entries. Models of the Space Needle seemed to be the big favorite. There were Space Needles made of Popsicle sticks, Space Needles made of clothespins, even a Space Needle cake. None of them looked like very tough competition.

But when I got to the last Space Needle, I paused. And stared. It was spectacular. It was almost four feet tall and made the other Space Needles look like Tinker Toys. It almost made the *real* Space Needle look like a Tinker Toy. Whoever had built it had a great career waiting at NASA.

Then I glanced at the name on the entry form: Cam Davis.

"Some of those other projects looked pretty good," I remarked as Nelson and I walked back down the hall. "Will you mind terribly if we don't win?"

"Of course I will," Nelson said. He sounded fairly cheerful about it. "But I think it's been worth it. In the long run."

I peered at Nelson. I suddenly wondered if you were supposed to invite people to restaurant openings when they had a crush on you and you didn't know how you felt about it.

Since I wasn't sure, I did what I always do. I opened my big mouth.

"Nelson, would you consider coming to the grand opening of my mom's restaurant tonight? It's called the

Golden Groat, and this crummy band, the Paramedics, is playing, and the whole thing will probably be very boring, but . . ."

Nelson squinted at me. "Do I have to get another haircut?" he asked. "That was your last condition, if I recall."

"No," I said. "Just come as you are, Nelson."

As he reached for the door of the station wagon, his smile was positively reptilian. "I think I can handle that one," he said.

After Nelson and his mother dropped me off at the restaurant, I found Sally flying around the kitchen, unpacking boxes of food and counting the silverware. My father was stacking a pile of menus fresh from the printer, and Pru was nowhere in sight.

I stood in the middle of the dining room and looked around. I had to hand it to Hurricane Sally. Even though she acted weird and embarrassing sometimes —even though she didn't like people to wear makeup or shave their legs and had even let her baby daughter teethe on a purple dinosaur—when it came to the Golden Groat, she had really outdone herself.

The whitewashed walls were decorated with framed prints of French Impressionist paintings. I'm not a huge Impressionist fan, but I had to admit they added a nice Continental touch. Baskets of flowers hung from the beams of the ceiling. Each table was covered with a very expensive red-and-white Sur La Table tablecloth.

"Where's the sign, Dad?" I asked, as he shoved a box

of candlesticks in my hands and pointed to the tables. "How will anybody know what this place is?"

"Don't worry," he said. "The guy from the sign place just called. He promised us it would be up by the time the doors open." He paused and stared at a scribbled list. "Oh, Lord, I forgot to fill the water pitchers," he sighed, and hurried off to the kitchen.

By the time I'd finished setting out the candlesticks, swept the floor, and taste-tested the creamy yogurt salad dressing, Pru still hadn't shown up. I folded the last napkin into a pointed triangle and glanced at my mother. "I'm sure she's waiting at home," I said. "She probably just forgot."

Sally sighed. She had pulled her red hair into a knot and shoved a pencil through it. She was looking a little frazzled. "Listen," she said, "why don't you jump on the bus and go get changed? And tell your sister she has some extra KP duty coming for not being here on time." She hoisted a carton of broccoli and began to haul it back to the sink. "We'll pick you up in about an hour. And put on something nice, in case any photographers come tonight." She looked excited at the idea.

"Okay, Mom." I helped her carry the rest of the stuff out to the kitchen. Then I raced out the door and down the street to the bus stop.

The first thing I noticed when I got home was that the house was empty. The next thing I noticed was that the phone was ringing. I picked it up on the fifth ring. It was Heather.

"Hi," she said. "I just called to see if you guys need a ride over to the Golden Groat."

"Thanks, anyway," I said, "but I just came back to change clothes. My parents said they'd pick us up. Listen," I added, "is Pru over there? She didn't show up at the Groat, and I haven't seen her since math."

"I haven't either," Heather said. "But if she shows up, I'll tell her you were looking for her."

Then I heard someone call Heather's name. "Hey, I have to go. We're in the middle of making sushi. Wait'll you taste it, Mattie. It's incredible!"

"I've tasted sushi," I said. "Incredible isn't exactly the word I'd use for it."

"That was your mother's sushi," Heather said tactfully. "Wait until you try the real thing." She turned away from the phone and called, "Just a minute, Mom!"

"I'll see you tonight," I told Heather and went off to hunt up a clean blouse.

As I was digging through the closet, I noticed *Mary, Queen of Scots* lying under some old tennis shoes.

I picked up the book and dusted it off. Maybe I could get in a few chapters before Pru got home. She was probably over at Lydia's, learning how to put on false eyelashes and underwire training bras.

Pretty soon she'd probably start smoking cigarettes. And shoplifting. Yes, I thought, as I lay down on the bed, definitely shoplifting. And hanging out in front of the Animal Cage with guys who wore skull-andcrossbone jackets, and riding around on the back of motorcycles. And smuggling drugs.

I suddenly remembered a show about juvenile delinquency I'd seen on public TV. It was called "A Cry for Help" and it was narrated by one of the actors from *M*A*S*H*. He looked straight into the camera and explained that when delinquents acted obnoxious, they were really just begging for help. And that the people who ignored their obnoxiousness were actually pushing them closer to a life of crime.

I could still hear the earnest way he'd said that. Poor Pru, I thought. She certainly had a horrible future to look forward to.

But maybe it wasn't too late. As soon as she got home, I'd explain to Pru that her obnoxious behavior was really a cry for help. And then I'd describe the peer counseling and the halfway houses that the *M*A*S*H* guy had talked about.

I hoped there were some decent halfway houses in the neighborhood. We could go visit Pru once a week, and she'd be so relieved that her cry for help had been heard, she wouldn't even mind when I took down that dumb *National Velvet* wallpaper and moved her bed up to the attic.

Picturing that made me feel a lot better. I flopped on my stomach and opened the book.

I had just found my place when I heard a noise. I sat still and listened. It was the sound of someone knocking. I jumped off the bed and ran downstairs.

When I opened the kitchen door, Cam Davis stood on the back steps. He smiled uncertainly. "Listen," he said. "This will probably sound kind of strange, but my mom needs to see you right away. She has a message for you."

"A message?" I snorted. "Who from? King Tut?"

Cam shook his head. "She wouldn't tell me. She just said to come get you. And that it was very important."

I peered at Cam. He didn't seem to be kidding. "Well, okay," I said, "but I can't stay long." I scribbled a note and left it on the kitchen table. Then I followed Cam down the back steps and around the hedge.

Chloe was in the living room, her crystals and pyramids spread in a circle in front of her. When she saw me, a look of relief crossed her face. "Good!" she said. "You've come."

She leaned forward. "Now, listen carefully. Earlier today I promised your mom I would contact the spirits to see how the restaurant opening would go. But for some reason, the channel was blocked. And then . . ."

Chloe held up a strangely shaped stone and stared at it. "Out of nowhere, I received the voice of Princess Mara. Princess Mara of ancient Egypt, your sister's spirit guide!"

"Princess Mara?" I tried not to laugh. "But that's impossible!"

Chloe frowned. "Impossible?"

I sighed. "Look, Pru made up that junk about Princess Mara to impress you. I'm sorry, but it's true. She

158

might as well have contacted the spirit of Elvis." I tried to look apologetic. "If you want to know the truth, my sister is about as spiritually gifted as an electric blender."

"Be that as it may," Chloe said, "I am telling you that I contacted your sister's spirit guide. I didn't understand everything she told me. The spirits often use cryptic clues to deliver their messages, you know."

She reached over and grabbed my hand. "But one thing came through that you must believe: your sister Prunehilda is in clear and present danger!"

And with that, every light in the Davises' house went out.

After a moment I heard Cam say, "Don't anybody move. I'll go check the circuit breaker." A second later, the lights came back on. "Must have been a power surge," he called. "That happens a lot in these old houses."

I looked at Chloe. "If that stuff about Pru was supposed to be a joke, I don't think it's very funny."

"It's no joke." Chloe picked up a scrap of paper and handed it to me. "Here—I wrote down everything the spirit said."

I squinted at the scribbling. "'A river of serpents'? 'The key to the crypt'? 'Through the eye of the needle'? What's that supposed to mean?"

"Maybe it's the Space Needle," Cam said from the kitchen door. "Maybe it's trying to tell us where Pru went."

"What on earth would Pru be doing at the Space Needle?" I stood up. "Listen," I said, "thanks for the warning. I'll let you know the minute she shows up."

"But she won't show up, don't you see?" Chloe jumped to her feet too. "If the spirit clues aren't any help, we'll just have to tap that famous ESP of yours. Quick now," Chloe said excitedly, "are you getting any mental images?"

I began backing toward the door. "I told you, we don't have ESP. And I really do have to get home. My mom and dad will be back any minute."

Just as I reached the door, it opened. But it was only Zee. She stared at me for a moment and looked around the room. "What's going on?" she asked. "Heavy-duty channeling session or something?"

"One of the twins is missing," Chloe announced, "and we're trying to figure out where she might be. You see, Princess Mara—"

Zee looked puzzled. "But I just saw her, maybe an hour ago? She was with that girl, the one with the leather bikini. Anyway, they drove past in this old car like the one your dad has. What is it?" Zee paused vaguely. "A Thunderbird or something?"

For a moment I couldn't breathe. "You mean, the Mustang?"

Zee shrugged. "Anyway, they were in this old car, bombing down Queen Anne Hill. I waved and junk, but I don't think they saw me."

A thin glaze of sweat broke out on the back of my

160

neck. "I'll be right back," I said. I raced out the door, heading for the garage.

When I reached the driveway, Cam was right behind me. For a moment we just stood there. Then Cam tugged at the heavy garage door, and we peered inside.

It was empty. The Mustang was gone, and so was Pru.

I turned to Cam. "I think we'd better find them before the police do," I said.

He squinted at me. "The police?"

"How many eighth graders do you know with a valid driver's license?"

"You're right," Cam said. "We'd better find them. Wait right here. I'll go get my bike."

That's when I remembered Nelson. He'd be showing up any minute. "Okay," I said, "but I have to call Nelson first. Can I meet you out front?"

"Sure," he said. "But if he's coming along, you'd better tell him to bring a bike." And before I could say a word, Cam had slipped back through the hedge.

I headed for the house and the telephone. But first I checked the garage again, in case the Mustang had magically reappeared.

It hadn't. As I gazed at the empty garage, a shiver went through me. Good old Prunehilda had really done it this time.

Ten minutes later, Nelson arrived. "Don't worry," he said briskly. "We'll find her."

Then he paused, and his face looked stern. "Maybe we should call the State Patrol. Lydia and Pru might have gotten on the Interstate, in which case we'll never find them."

"The freeway? They can't have gone that far." I tried not to picture the Mustang zooming toward Portland. Or Las Vegas, for that matter. "Pru doesn't even know how to use a gas pump. How far could they get on one measly tank of gas?"

"Far enough," Nelson said grimly. "Come on, give me your sister's bike, and let's get going."

"Nelson?" I paused uncomfortably. "Is it all right if someone else comes along?"

He frowned. "Someone else? Who, for instance?"

"Well, Cam Davis. He lives next door, and he has his own bike, and he offered to help us look." I felt like Sally trying to sell my father on Sur La Table tablecloths.

Nelson shrugged. "The more, the merrier," he said. But I could tell he didn't think it was all right.

Cam's ten-speed was poised in front of the house. He nodded when he saw Nelson. Then he turned to me.

"Okay, you're the local. Are there any drive-ins, hang-outs, places where a dip-brain like Lydia would go? You know, to show off the car?"

At the word "dip-brain," I stared at Cam. But Nelson broke in. "Personally, I think the drive-in's a good bet. We could start with that burger place down by the Center."

162

He and Cam jumped on their bikes. "Hey, wait," I said. "What about my parents? They're coming back to take us to the Golden Groat."

"My mom's going over there in a few minutes," Cam said. "I told her to try and stall them until we get back."

I glanced at Cam and Nelson. Their faces looked grim. Feeling like Mary, Queen of Scots, on her last trip to the Tower, I climbed on my bike and pushed off down the drive.

The Bun 'n' Burger was in an orange building at the bottom of the hill. I stared at the cars full of high school kids parked outside.

"Now what?" I said. "Do we just walk up to people and ask if they've seen two thirteen-year-old girls driving a '65 Mustang?"

The boys glanced at each other. "Sounds good to me," Cam said. "We'll ask around. Why don't you go inside and see if they ordered anything?"

I watched them walk over to a group of cars. Leaning my bike against the building, I pushed open the glass door and marched up to the counter.

A boy in a paper hat was filling the deep-fryer. I waited while he emptied a bag of french fries into the bubbling oil. Then he turned around, and I saw it was Robert, the boy from the ice-cream stand. The boy I'd worshiped for one entire summer.

He stared at me politely. "Yes? May I help you?"

I stared back. It was Robert, all right, but under the

fluorescent lights his blond hair looked darker, and his face, shiny from the fryer, showed the beginnings of definite skin problems.

Then I looked closer, and I couldn't believe my eyes. Robert, the ice-cream boy of my dreams, was wearing tawny beige cover-up to hide his acne.

I swallowed. "Hi," I said. "Remember me?" I paused. "From the lake this summer?"

Robert was gazing at me blankly. Oh, great, I thought. As if he hadn't met nine million girls at the lake. As if he'd remember some thirteen-year-old misfit, lurking in the shadows like a lovesick barber pole.

On second thought, maybe it was better if Robert didn't recognize me.

But it was too late. He was smiling. "Sure," he said. "You're one of the twins. Except you got your hair cut, right? How you doing?"

Incredible, I thought. Robert remembered me. He even remembered my hair.

"Actually," I said, "I was looking for my sister. I thought she might have come in here. With a tall blond girl?"

Robert looked doubtful. "Gee, we get a lot of kids in here after school. I'm not sure—" he started to say, when Cam and Nelson burst through the door.

"They were here," Nelson announced triumphantly. "And Lydia was driving the Mustang!"

"Someone thought they took off for the lake," Cam added. He turned, ready to sprint for his bike.

But I didn't move.

"What is it?" Nelson asked.

"Nothing." I paused. "It's just that . . . I don't think they went to the lake."

It wasn't ESP, I told myself. But right at that moment I knew where Pru had gone.

And I knew what must have happened. Lydia had talked Pru into taking the keys to the car. And then, before she knew it, they were heading for the drive-in.

But even Lydia couldn't have talked Pru into going any farther. They must have started back. So, if they were still missing . . .

"I have a feeling," I said, "that they've broken down. Somewhere between here and the house."

Cam peered at me suspiciously. "Does this have anything to do with that spirit guide stuff?" he asked.

"No," I said. "But you have to admit it was right about the Needle. It's practically across the street."

Nelson looked irritated. "What is this?" he asked, sticking his face between me and Cam. "A scavenger hunt?"

"No," I sighed, "but it's a long story."

"Well, what about the river of serpents?" Cam said. "That could mean the lake. There might be a serpent or two living down there," he added hopefully.

I shook my head. "I'm telling you, I know where she went—the Mount Saint Helens House!"

Cam stared at me impatiently. I could tell he was itching to head over to the lake and check for serpents.

"It's this old mansion right at the top of the hill," I said. "It was a mountain-climbing headquarters before the mountain blew up. Anyway," I added, "Pru and I used to have this dumb club, and we'd sneak over the wall to hold meetings and stuff." I decided to skip the part about the marshmallows.

"What makes you so sure she's there?" Cam asked.

"Because," I said, "that's where I would go if I was scared and needed a place to hide. And because . . ." I looked at him helplessly. "Because she's my sister."

Cam studied me for a moment. "It's worth a shot," he said. "Let's go."

"Hang on." Robert had been watching us from behind the counter. Suddenly he ducked into the kitchen. He came back and handed me a flashlight. "That place hasn't been open in years," he said. "It's pretty overgrown. I wouldn't get caught trespassing if I were you guys."

"We won't," I promised.

Robert nodded. "Let me know if you find her. And don't forget to return the flashlight. I need it to clean up the parking lot at closing."

"I'll guard it with my life." Clutching the flashlight, I hurried outside, where Cam and Nelson were waiting on their bikes.

"One point," Nelson said, as we were about to take off. "What do we do if they're not there?"

Everyone was silent for a moment.

Then Cam said, "We'll have to go back and report

them missing. But if Mattie's right and they've broken down, the police will have found them by now, anyway. So I vote we head for the mansion."

It was cold as we pedaled back up the hill. The wind cut through my sweater and brought water stinging to my eyes. But I gripped the handlebars and pedaled harder.

When we reached the top, Cam stared at the dark road that cut through the trees. "Look," he said, "there's the sign. 'Mount Saint Helens House.'" He paused and peered at the black mansion silhouetted against the sky. "Kinda spooky, isn't it?"

"There's no chain across the road," Nelson pointed out. "It would be easy to drive in here, if—"

"If the police had spotted you and you didn't have a license." I looked around. Robert was right. The ancient firs behind the mansion had grown so dense you could hardly see three feet in front of you. I reached into my bike basket and grabbed the flashlight. Following the beam of light, we started down the path, the bicycle tires crunching on a thick carpet of pine needles.

Soon, the tall fir trees had cut off our view of the house. We moved slowly through the mansion grounds and over a ridge, where the path suddenly ended, swallowed up by leafy overgrowth.

I aimed the flashlight into the tangled branches. "It's no use," I said finally. "If they were here, we'd have found them. I guess we'd better head back."

Cam nodded grimly. "You want to check the lake?"

"I guess so." Then I stared down at the mossy ground. "I'm sorry. I was just so sure . . ."

Nelson patted my shoulder awkwardly. "Maybe she's back at the house, right now," he said. "Listen, it was worth a try."

"Yeah, sure," I said. But it didn't make me feel any better.

After a moment, the two boys turned their bikes around and began to push them up the path. I stayed behind, glaring into the woods.

"Thanks a lot, Prunehilda," I said. "You've definitely done it this time. And if anything's happened to you, I'll . . . I'll . . ." But for once I couldn't think up a decent threat.

I tried to tell myself that if Pru was in Las Vegas, I'd finally get my own room. I tried to tell myself that she was probably off having a great time somewhere. Maybe someday we'd get a postcard, addressed in Pru's perfect penmanship. "Having a wonderful life," it would say. "Wish you were here."

But it didn't work. Pru was gone, and the only thing I felt was awful.

"Are you coming?" Nelson asked.

"Yeah," I called. Slowly I swung my bike around. I was about to start trudging back up the path, when a small voice spoke up from the dark forest.

"Mattie? Is that you?"

It was Pru.

fifteen

~~~~~~

I peered into the shadows. "It's okay, Pru," I called. "It's just us." I paused. "Are you all right?"

I heard a small snuffle. Then Pru came out from behind a tree, blinking in the beam of the flashlight. "How did you find us?" she asked in a tiny voice. For once, she looked glad to see me.

"ESP," I said. And I socked her on the arm so she'd know it was me and not the ghost of Princess Mara.

Nelson cleared his throat. "I hate to sound practical," he said, "but—where's the car?"

There was a long silence. It was broken by the sound of Lydia Carthage crashing out of the woods. There was a black streak on her forehead, and her blond hair was full of leaves. "Are they gone?" she demanded.

"Is who gone?" Cam asked.

"The police." Pru looked as if she wanted to dive back into the bushes. "We were coming back from the drive-in when this police car started to follow us." She shuddered. "So I told Lydia to pull in here."

"And now the car won't start," Lydia announced. She pointed at the shadowy trees. "It's back there somewhere."

We followed Cam down a trail of crumpled branches. Finally he called out, "Here it is. Let's give the starter a try."

The Mustang had stopped a few inches from a gnarled pine at the edge of the clearing. Its gleaming turquoise paint wasn't gleaming anymore, and I thought it looked a little forlorn—embarrassed, even—to be out here in the middle of the woods instead of in a parking lot, getting drooled on by teenage boys.

Cam turned the key. A noise that sounded like my father's coffee grinder filled the clearing. "Bad news," Cam said after a few more tries. "It must be the electrical system."

Pru began to cry. "I've wrecked Daddy's caaar! He's going to kill meee!"

"It's not wrecked," Cam told her. "Don't worry, we'll get it out of here somehow."

He climbed out of the car and looked at Lydia. "That was a pretty dumb stunt you guys pulled," he said. "You could have gotten in big trouble."

Lydia gave him her blond lizard smile. "But we didn't, did we? We knew someone like you would rescue us," she said, batting her eyelashes.

Watching Lydia's eyelashes fluttering like trapped moths, I wished one of Nelson's Lambeosaurs would come strolling out of the woods and carry her away. I hoped Lambeosaurs had very sharp teeth.

Lydia tossed her head. "Well, it *was* fun. Wasn't it, Pru?"

Make that an extremely hungry Tyrannosaurus Rex. I scowled at Lydia, but everyone else had turned to look at Pru.

Pru scratched her nose doubtfully. "I wouldn't call it . . . fun, exactly," she said. "Besides, we still have to get the car out. I mean, we can't just leave it here."

Everyone looked back at Lydia. It was like watching a weird kind of tennis match. Lydia seemed to be trying to decide which was more important—saving her skin or getting in some more batting practice.

Finally she grabbed her purse off the front seat. "Look, I'm sorry, but my mom said I had to be home by six, and I'm probably late already." She waved impatiently at the Mustang. "Why don't you guys just call a tow truck or something? Come on, Pru, let's go."

Pru turned to face Lydia. She put her hands on her hips and stuck out her chin. Normally I hated it when Pru did that, but I had to admit that under the circumstances it was effective.

"Lydia," she said, "I don't care if you told your mom you'd be home yesterday. I don't care if your dad is an airline pilot and you promised me a free trip to New York City. Swiping cars is *not* fun. And if you leave now," Pru said, "I will never, ever speak to you again." Game, set, and match.

There was silence in the clearing. Then Lydia shrugged. "Suit yourself," she said. A moment later, we heard her crashing back along the path.

Pru heaved a big sigh. "I'm glad that's over with," she said. "She was driving me nuts. Now—can we please get out of here?"

We decided to push the car out of the woods. "We might even get it back to your house," Cam said, "as long as nobody sees us. You want to steer, Pru?"

Pru shook her head. "I never want to set foot in that thing again!"

"In that case," Cam said, "it looks like your sister's elected. Just aim it at the middle of the road," he told me, "and leave the driving to us."

I climbed behind the wheel and stared at the pedals. Dread clawed its way through my stomach, looking for a place to hide. Waves of fear hammered at my chest as I studied the dials and gauges on the dashboard. I didn't know how to drive. I didn't *want* to know how to drive. If we got out of this alive, I was definitely going to have to kill Pru, just on principle.

Then the car gave a jerk, and the tires began to roll over the soggy ground, back up to the rutted road. Branches loomed out of nowhere and lashed against the windshield. I clung to the steering wheel as the car jounced slowly along the path.

Suddenly a movement behind me caught my eye. "Hey, you kids!" a hoarse voice shouted. "What are you doing in there?"

I peered into the rear-view mirror. A very angry-looking man stood in the door of the Mount Saint Helens House, frowning and peering into the trees.

I leaned out the window. "Can't you hurry it up? I'm not exactly invisible here, you know."

"We're almost to the gate," Cam called. "Just a few more yards to go."

The man began to march down the mansion steps. The next minute, he caught sight of the car and broke into a run.

At the same moment, the tires hit a rut and stopped. In a minute the man would reach us, and then we would be arrested, and our pictures would be splashed on the front page of the *Queen Anne Gazette,* right next to a Bev Adams editorial on the tragedy of juvenile delinquency. We would have to go live in a halfway house and. . . .

The Mustang rolled free. The gates of the mansion loomed up in front of me, and I clutched the wheel.

"You kids stay out of here!" the man yelled. But we were already through the gates, heading for the street.

It was downhill to McIntire Street. Even so, when we reached our block, my hands ached and my neck felt stiff. Finally the Mustang coasted to a stop at the corner.

I was just about to jump out of the car, when a blue pick-up truck pulled up next to my window.

"Battery die on you folks?" the driver called. "Say, I'd be glad to give you a push."

I peeked over the steering wheel, praying the man would go away. Firmly I shook my head. Maybe he'd figure I was a friendly young deaf-mute, or a foreign exchange student, out pushing a car around with a bunch of friends.

The man was peering at me suspiciously. "Hey, girlie, are you all right?" By now he had probably noticed I was pretty young to be peeking over the wheel of a Mustang. TEEN MUTE NABBED IN HIGH-SPEED CHASE, Bev Adams's headline would read. LOCAL JOYRIDE ENDS IN TRAGEDY. I slipped down in the seat until my head was practically under the wheel.

"We only have one more block to go, sir," I heard Cam say. "But thanks, anyway."

He waited until the pick-up truck had driven off before jogging up to the window. "We'll give you one more shove. You can coast the rest of the way from here," he told me. "Nelson and I are going back for the bikes."

Pru was standing in the middle of the street, looking scared.

"Get in," I told her. "It'll be better if we present a united front. Kronis only knows what Chloe has been telling them."

"Chloe?"

"She got a message from Princess Mara that you were in trouble."

"Really? Princess Mara?" Pru looked incredulous.

But she walked over and got in. I took my foot off the brake, and the boys shoved.

As soon as the Mustang began to roll down McIntire Street, Cam headed up the hill with Nelson at his heels. "Don't get arrested," I yelled after them. Then I gripped the wheel and aimed the Mustang toward the house. "Well? Are you normal again? Free from the Lydia spell?"

Pru nodded. "I—"

Then her face turned blue. I watched in horror as Pru's face went from blue to red to blue again. I whirled around. Parked behind us was a patrol car, its lights revolving ominously.

"Oh, brother," I muttered. "It's the cops. It's really, truly the cops."

One by one, the doors of the patrol car swung open. Pru and I waited in silence as the two policemen walked up to the Mustang. One of them held a flashlight, which he shone on the license plate and into the backseat.

"It's okay," I told Pru. "They're probably looking for an escaped convict or something. They probably just want to ask if we've seen anything suspicious."

Pru swallowed hard. "Yeah, probably," she said, but she didn't sound too convinced.

There was a knock at my window. "Are you the owner of this vehicle, miss?" a deep voice asked.

I squinted into the flashlight beam. "Um, er . . .

in a way. I mean, my father is the owner. Of the vehicle."

The other policeman walked over to Pru's window. He was shorter and fatter than the first policeman, and he didn't seem to be in a very good mood. "This vehicle was observed driving up Queen Anne Hill earlier today," he said in a flat voice. "The reporting officer noted the license number and traced the registration to this address. He had reason to suspect the driver of the vehicle was underage."

No one said anything while Pru and I sat there looking underage. This was, I decided, the most horrible day of my life. All the headlines I'd pictured were about to come true. LOCAL TWINS NABBED IN UNDERAGE CAR HEIST: IDENTICAL FINGERPRINTS TELL A TRAGIC TALE. I glanced at Pru. Her bottom lip was starting to tremble. In another minute she'd burst into tears and confess the whole thing.

"Miss?" the taller policeman said. "Would you mind stepping out of the car?"

I peered up at him. "Aren't you supposed to read us our rights first?" I asked politely.

He smiled. "This isn't an arrest. We'd just like to ask you a few questions."

I was just trying to decide whether to turn myself in, when the front door of our house opened and my father came out. He walked over to my policeman, who was writing something down in a pad. "Afternoon, officers," he said in a friendly voice. "Anything I can help you with?"

"Good afternoon, sir," the officer said. "It looks like your kids here have been out for a little ride. A patrolman spotted them entering the grounds of a private estate about an hour ago. In this car." He tapped his pencil against the pad and stared impassively at my father.

Dad stared impassively back. "I don't see how that's possible, officer," he said. "My car isn't running. Must have left the lights on overnight," he added apologetically. "It's been sitting here ever since."

The policeman nodded slowly. "Well, I'm sure that's the case, sir. But just for the sake of investigation, would you mind giving the engine a try?"

My father shrugged. "No problem at all," he said. "But unless my daughters took a ride over to Sears for a new battery, I don't think it's going to start," he added, laughing nervously.

The policeman gave him a sharp look. My father stopped laughing and motioned us out of the car. "Come on, kids," he said in a loud voice. "You've been sitting out here long enough. Probably sneaking a smoke," he added to the policemen. They smiled.

Pru huddled next to the shorter policeman, staring at his gun. All four of us watched as my father got in the car, adjusted the seat, and turned the key.

I heard the coffee-grinder noise once and then twice.

With a flourish, my father turned the key again. Nothing.

He shrugged. "Looks like I'll have to get someone out here to jump-start it."

"We can radio for a tow truck, sir," the policeman said.

My father climbed hastily out of the car. "No, no, that's perfectly all right," he said. "I'll have someone come out first thing in the morning. Now, is there anything else I can do for you?"

The policeman switched off his flashlight. He shut his pad. "No, that's fine. Sorry for the inconvenience, sir. Just doing our job." He touched his hat and followed his partner back to the patrol car. Pru and I watched as they murmured into their radios. Then the blue and red lights went out, and the police car drove away.

My father waited until they were gone. Then he turned to us. "Are you all right?" he asked in a grim voice.

Pru nodded, miserable. She took a deep breath. "Lydia said her father lets her drive all the time. She promised we'd just go up and down the street. But it was all a big lie. And I'll never do it again, so please don't kill me. And I'm sorry the car broke down," Pru added, her lower lip starting to tremble again.

"Well, I'm not," my father remarked, hugging Pru firmly. Then he hugged me for good measure. "Otherwise, you and what's-her-name might be halfway to the state line by now. What was that kid planning to do, anyway? Sell my car and hightail it to Rio?"

He shook his head and began to inspect the Mustang. "Looks like I've got my work cut out for me," he muttered, examining the scratched paint. But I noticed he didn't sound too upset about it.

I followed him around the side of the car. "Wasn't that obstructing justice, what you did just now?" I asked. "I mean, you *lied* to a policeman. You always told us we were never, ever supposed to—"

My father interrupted me sternly. "I meant that. You should never lie to a policeman to cover up a crime. However, in this instance, I considered my first duty was to my daughters. I didn't raise you to be criminals, and I acted on that assumption. But I'd appreciate not being put in this position again."

Then he shrugged. "Of course, if you'd prefer, Mattie, I can have them come back and book you. One grand theft auto felony, coming right up."

"That's okay," I said quickly. "Actually, I thought you were quite magnificent."

"Thank you," he said. "I thought so too." Then he lifted the hood and fiddled with something in the engine. A moment later, he climbed in the car and turned the key. It started right up.

My father listened to the engine purr with a satisfied smile. "There's a little wire that shakes loose every once in a while. I figured you kids couldn't have gotten too far." He patted the dashboard affectionately. "Just a little built-in anti-theft insurance," he said, as Cam came riding up the drive, steering my bike with one hand while Nelson followed behind on Pru's.

"Boy," Cam said, "we got out of there just in time. That old castle was lit up like a Christmas tree. Cops everywhere!"

"We snuck in through the park and grabbed the bikes," Nelson added. His thin face was flushed with excitement.

My father looked at the boys. Then he looked at us. "Tell me later," he said. "Or sooner. Your mother's waiting for us at the restaurant." Putting the Mustang in gear, he drove it into the garage.

Cam and Nelson watched him silently. "It has a built-in anti-theft device," I told them. "Did you remember to bring the flashlight?"

"It's right here in your basket," Cam said. "Maybe we can drop it off on the way to the restaurant."

For a moment I felt a pang of excitement. The flashlight would be a good excuse to see Robert again. Then I caught myself. I didn't need some dumb excuse to see Robert if I felt like it. Except maybe a cheeseburger deluxe with extra pickles.

"Listen," I said to Nelson, as Cam went to inspect the Mustang's anti-theft device, "do you still want to come to the opening of the Golden Groat? We were supposed to be there hours ago. Besides," I added, "I did invite you."

Nelson nodded. "That's true," he said. "You did."

I kicked at the gravel in the driveway, and a pebble hit him in the leg. "Nelson? You know, for your basic maladjusted eighth-grade genius, I thought you did okay today."

Nelson paused. "Well, thanks, Darwin," he said finally. "For a stubborn, anxiety-ridden clone, you didn't do too badly yourself."

I smiled modestly. And then we were dashing for the Volvo.

sixteen

~~~~~~

As we rode down the hill, I sat in the backseat of the Volvo and stared at my sister's head. She was probably thinking how lucky we were to have a magnificently loyal and trusting father who didn't go bananas when someone stole his favorite possession in the world and who stuck up for his daughters when they were facing a possible grand theft auto.

I peeked over at Cam. A streetlight lit up his face, and I noticed for the thousandth time how cute his nose was and the adorable way his hair curled down over his forehead.

Oh well. In a few years he would probably get acne like Robert, and start plastering his face with tawny beige cover-up. Until then, I'd just have to suffer.

After we returned the flashlight to the Bun 'n' Burger, my father stopped at a 7-Eleven and bought two packages of paper plates. "Your mother sent me back to the house to get extras," he explained. "And a good thing too," he added meaningfully. "But just between you and me, it didn't look like she was going to need them." He shook his head. "If I told her once, I told her a thousand times — a restaurant is an extremely risky undertaking."

"You mean no one showed up?" I asked.

He sighed. "Just Mrs. Yamamoto, Heather, and the band. If you sit still, you can probably hear them from here."

Poor Mom, I thought. Not one lousy macrobiotic fan had shown up for her big opening. I tried not to picture her waiting hopefully while the Paramedics screamed away in the background. It was too awful.

"Maybe people in Seattle like to eat late," Pru suggested.

"That's right," Nelson said, as we passed the Seattle Center and headed for Bell Street. "She'll probably have better luck once the movies let out."

"Oh, come on, Nelson," I said. "Since when have you gone to the movies and then rushed right out for brown rice and bean sprouts?"

Nelson paused. "I usually buy a jumbo tub of buttered popcorn when I go to the movies," he said.

"Then I imagine you usually feel pretty sick."

"That's true," Nelson replied. "But I usually have to eat it all by myself." He gave me a direct stare. I blushed and looked away.

"Well, you were right about the band," Cam

remarked, as my father parked the car. "I can definitely hear them from here."

Pru was peering up the street. She gave my father a puzzled look. "I thought you said no one showed up."

At the end of the block, a crowd of people milled around the door of a brightly lit storefront. My father was peering at them too. He scratched his beard in amazement. "God only knows what was playing at the movies," he muttered.

"Maybe it was a Woody Allen movie," Pru suggested. "Woody Allen would probably remind people of bean sprouts."

No one had an answer for that, so we got out and began walking toward the crowd. Then I noticed the sign over the door: "The Golden Goat."

Nelson nudged me. "Is that anything like the Trojan Horse?"

"The signmaker got the name wrong," my father explained. He was still gazing around at the crowd. "He offered to fix it for free. But after tonight, we may be stuck with it. Based on what I'm seeing, I'd say the Golden Goat was a culinary hit."

Grinning, he stepped through the door, and the rest of us followed him inside.

At the end of the crowded room my mother stood guard over a long table of diners' co-op entries. In front of the table, Mrs. Yamamoto and Chloe were discussing the merits of sushi versus octopus. Nearby, Lyle was explaining the importance of software to Heather's uncle, who was scribbling notes on the back of a menu. Zee and the Paramedics sprawled near the kitchen door, taking a break between sets.

"Well, what do you think?" I asked Nelson.

"I like it," he said. "It's . . ." Then he stopped. "Mom? What are *you* doing here?"

Mrs. Richfield sat at a small table, sampling a piece of rhubarb pie. She looked up and smiled. "You didn't expect me to wait outside in the car, did you? Hello, Mattie." She pointed at her plate appreciatively. "I can highly recommend the pie."

Then she winced. "I'm sorry, I forgot all about your food allergies." She gave me a sympathetic smile. "Everything here is so delicious. I hope there's something you can eat."

My face turned bright red. I was just about to explain that they were really very *mild* food allergies, when Heather marched up.

"Mattie! Where have you guys been? Your mom was ready to call the cops!"

"She didn't have to," I said. "They already found us."

"What?"

"Never mind," I said. "Come on, let's go get some sushi."

We pushed through the crowd—past Bev Adams, who was scribbling down a rave review for the *Queen*

Anne Gazette, her shark's tooth earrings clattering; past Pru, who was grilling Chloe about Princess Mara; past Cam, who was telling his sister about our adventure in the woods—and headed for the food table.

"So what's been going on?" I asked Heather.

"Well, for one thing, you missed most of the decent food. Someone even made French pastries, but your mom disqualified them from the co-op contest because she said they promoted the use of refined sugar."

"That figures," I said. But I noticed that all the French pastries were gone.

"And then this guy from the Italian restaurant down the street showed up and started playing his violin at all the tables, so my dad made me get up and play this Hungarian rhapsody. It was really awful." Heather beamed.

"How come you look so happy if you screwed up?"

"Because," Heather said, "right after that, one of the Paramedics came up and told me they loved my sound, and had I ever considered joining a band."

"Heather! You didn't—"

"Of course not," Heather smiled. "But when I told him I was planning to become a fashion designer, he asked if I'd like to do some clothes for the band. Because if my fashions were anything like my violin playing, they were just what the Paramedics were looking for!"

"Gee, Heather," I said, "I'm not sure I'd consider that a compliment. But he's right. This might be just what the world has been waiting for: avant-garde emergency-room fashion. And now, before you break any more news, let's get some of this food."

But just as I reached for a plate, someone tapped me on the arm. "Excuse me. Do you know where we enter our recipes for the contest?"

A friendly looking woman with short blond hair stood holding a platter wrapped in waxed paper. "I heard about this diner's cooperative thing, and it sounded so interesting, I just had to bring my daughter. And my Swedish meatballs," she added, brandishing the plate. "My grandmother's recipe."

"Talk to that red-headed woman over there," I said. "She's the owner. I understand she studied at the Paris Academy of Cooking. Makes all the desserts herself."

The woman beamed and turned to someone beside her. "Isn't this fun? And look at all the food, Liddie! It's like those old-fashioned smorgasbords I was telling you about."

I glanced past the woman at the newest member of the Golden Goat cooperative, and for a minute I didn't know whether to start laughing or grab a handful of sushi and take aim. Because there, staring miserably at the platter of Swedish meatballs, was Lydia Carthage.

After the restaurant had closed, Heather and I sat at one of the tables and discussed the night's weirder moments.

"The part I couldn't believe," Heather said, "was

when Ramon and that Animal Cage girl showed up."

"Don't forget, his cousin is a Paramedic."

"I know," Heather said. "But what was that stuff they brought? Pink and green Jell-O salad?"

I watched Lyle and my father stack the chairs so that Cam could sweep under the tables. "You're right," I said. "That was pretty weird."

But the weirdest part of the whole night was Lydia. Maybe all that stuff Sally claimed about health food was true, that it made people less aggressive. Or maybe Lydia was just in shock at seeing us alive and well. Whatever the reason, when one of the Paramedics walked up and tried to talk to her, Lydia ducked her head and hid behind her mother. I couldn't get over it. Under her blond reptile disguise, Lydia Carthage was nothing but a golden sheep. On second thought, make that a goat.

At the end of the night, Sally announced the winning dish, a recipe for mulligan stew entered by an off-duty cop. As I watched him go up to receive his prize—a coupon good for two free dinners at the Golden Goat—I felt like hiding behind Lydia's mother too.

"I never want to see another policeman as long as I live," I whispered to Pru. She and Lydia hadn't spoken to each other all night. I had to hand it to Prunehilda. When she made a promise, she kept it.

Pru shuddered. "I wonder what would have happened if Dad hadn't been there. Would they really have arrested us, do you think?"

"Don't talk about it," I said loyally. I handed her my plate. "Here, try some sushi. If you can forget what's in it, it doesn't taste half-bad."

Believe it or not, it didn't.

seventeen

By the time we made it to bed, we were full of sushi, and sore from shoving the Mustang around, and tired from all the talk and excitement. Downstairs, our parents and the Davises and the Sawyers sat in the kitchen, discussing politics and land values and the future of software. Someone, Sally probably, had put on the Beatles' *Rubber Soul* album, and the music drifted up the stairwell, lulling me to sleep.

"Mattie?" Pru whispered. "Are you still awake?"

"Mmm."

There was a pause. Then Pru said, "That was funny when Chloe admitted that she saw us take the car. She knew about it all along!"

"Yeah," I said. "So how come she still claims Princess Mara was behind the whole thing? I mean, she practically convinced me you'd been swallowed up by a river of snakes!"

Pru propped herself on one elbow. "She probably didn't want it to affect her sales," she said.

"What sales?"

"*The Sounds of Sunset*. Didn't you see them? Mom had them displayed next to the cash register."

I rolled over on my stomach. "Does this mean you finally admit that Princess Mara was a hoax?"

Pru squirmed under the blanket. "I wouldn't use the word 'hoax,'" she said at last. "I definitely think 'hoax' is the wrong—"

"Never mind," I said. "Good-night, Pru."

I was three-fifths asleep when Pru's voice came drifting across the room again. "Mattie?" she whispered. "Did you notice anything weird tonight? At the restaurant?"

"I'll say—that green Jell-O! It had all these little pink things in it, and—"

"I don't mean the food," Pru said. "I mean, did you notice that not one person—not *one*—came up and asked us if we were twins?"

I thought about it. "That's true," I said. "They were probably too busy eating sushi. Or listening to Dad play "My Way" on the electric piano. Which was about the grossest thing I've ever heard." Then I remembered Zee's singing. "Well, almost the grossest."

I closed my eyes again. Then I heard: "Mattie?"

"What?"

"Sometimes . . . sometimes I wish we weren't twins."

My eyes flew open. "Really? You do?"

"Yes," Pru said. She paused. "Don't you?"

I remembered wishing I could divorce Pru on the grounds of incompatibility. "Well, I wouldn't go out and get a face transplant, just because we look alike."

"I mean," Pru went on, "I don't ever want to be one of those twins who live together their whole lives. You know, the ones who wear the same little hats and coats and shoes until they're practically a hundred years old?"

"Me neither," I said. I was getting very sleepy. "But you can't expect people to tell us apart unless we try to do stuff on our own."

"I know," Pru said, but she didn't sound happy about it. "That's why I tried to be friends with Lydia. It wasn't much fun, though. Not being a twin was harder than I thought."

The Beatles were singing "Michelle." I got up and sat on the foot of Pru's bed. "We don't have to stop being twins," I said. "But maybe . . . we could give it a rest once in a while."

"What do you mean?"

"We could try not to fight so much, for one thing. I mean, if two totally incompatible people like Mom and Dad can get along, it can't be impossible." I paused. "And we could let people get to know us a little better. Without all the twin junk."

Pru was silent for a moment. "But how do I know people will like me if I'm just *me*?" she said finally.

I curled up on her bed and pulled some of the blanket

over my shoulders. "Some of them will, Pru. Honest."

"But maybe some of them won't!"

I patted her foot. "Maybe not," I said sleepily. "But you'll still have me, and Heather, and Mom and Dad . . ." My eyes were closing by themselves now, and there was nothing I could do about it.

Pru poked me under the covers. "Mattie? Are you still awake?"

"Mmm."

"I was just wondering. Would you be mad if . . . I got my hair cut? I don't mean exactly like yours," Pru said quickly. "But—"

"Just don't go near the Animal Cage," I mumbled. "And if you do, stay away from a guy named Ramon."

"Mattie?"

"Yes, Prune."

"Good-night, Mattie."

"Mmm." Which is what you say when you're 99.8 percent asleep.

On Wednesday, the weather was wet and cold, and I woke up late. I was already in a bad mood by the time I got to school. My mood didn't improve when I saw Nelson's face.

"I heard a rumor, Darwin," he said grimly. "I think this is it. D-Day. As in Dino-Rama."

Butterflies the size of Pterodactyls invaded my stomach. "Are you sure?"

"I heard Mrs. B. on the phone, talking to the news-paper. And I don't think she was ordering a subscrip-tion."

"The newspaper? Does that mean someone from our school won?"

"Maybe us," Nelson said in a dire voice. "And maybe not."

We looked at each other. "Let's go find Mr. Gruen-feld," I said.

The art room was crowded by the time we got there. As soon as we found seats, Mr. Gruenfeld got up and closed the door.

"One first prize," he announced, "one third, and two honorable mentions. Not bad for a school our size."

Nelson nudged me. He was looking insufferably confident, which, I knew, meant he was even more ner-vous than I was.

"Nelson," I whispered. "Will you still speak to me if we don't win?"

His grin faded. "Number one," he whispered back, "I didn't get you into this so we could cop a third. Number two, I dropped four games of postal chess because of you, so I guess you're stuck with me. Now sit up straight. He's about to call our names."

The room was silent as Mr. Gruenfeld tore open the envelope. He studied the results for a moment. Then he smiled.

"I'm pleased to announce that first prize, a three-hundred-dollar Wyndham's gift certificate and free passes to all Seattle Center facilities, goes to Cameron Davis for his model of the Space Needle. Third prize . . ."

But I wasn't listening anymore. I was looking at Nelson. His face had turned a horrible shade of green.

". . . and honorable mention goes to the team of Darwin and Richfield, for their imaginative Dino-Rama," Mr. Gruenfeld said, still reading off the results.

Nelson smiled wanly. "Gee, honorable mention," he said. "I told you we wouldn't cop a third."

People began to gather around Cam, congratulating him. But Mr. Gruenfeld was waving his hand in the air. "I've got one more announcement before we finish up here," he called.

He studied the paper in his hand and scratched his head. "It says here that the Pacific Science Center wants to purchase Darwin and Richfield's diorama." The teacher grinned. "Must have liked the subject matter. At any rate, they want to exhibit it with their animated dinosaur display when it travels to Spokane next year."

"Huh?" Nelson's eyes suddenly focused. "What'd he say?"

I grabbed his arm. "You said they wouldn't be able to resist the Dino-Rama. And you were right, Nelson! They want to buy it!"

"They do? How much?" Nelson called out.

"I'm sure that can be worked out with your agent, Mr. Richfield," the art teacher said drily. "But congratulations. You both did a fine job."

"Just think," Nelson said, "our Dino-Rama, enshrined for posterity. That beats some crummy old gift certificate any day." Some of his smugness was starting to return. It was, I thought, a good sign.

Then photographers from the newspaper arrived to take Cam's picture, and Nelson and I were propped in front of the Dino-Rama, holding up the letter from the Science Center.

When the last flashbulb had popped, I turned to Nelson. "I'll be right back," I said. "There's something I have to do before assembly."

I reached in my pocket to see whether my new pearlescent primrose lipstick was still there. After a lot of thought, I'd decided flamingo-pink just wasn't my color. Still, I *was* thirteen. A person had to grow up sometime.

"Okay," Nelson said, "but don't take forever. This is our moment of glory, Darwin."

"I won't."

Pushing my way past the exhibits, I didn't notice that someone was following me. Then I broke free of the crowd and I saw Cam standing by the door.

He stared down at his sneakers. "Listen," he said, "I thought your project was great. It should have won, hands down."

"Thanks," I said, "but everything worked out okay. Nelson's convinced that the Dino-Rama will be enshrined for posterity."

Cam gave me a long look, and I wondered if my hair

was sticking up again. Now that it had grown out a little, it did that sometimes.

Cam cleared his throat. "Do you think Nelson would mind if I invited you to see *Revenge of the Zombies*? I mean, it's the least I can do, considering the way you guys got gypped. And I'd invite old Nelson too," he went on, "except I only have these two passes. Some guy gave them to my dad, and . . ."

It suddenly occurred to me that Cam was asking me to the movies.

And what's more, he was acting very nervous about it. "Does that mean," I said carefully, "that Pru can't come either?"

Cam looked surprised. "You mean, *you're* not Pru?"

I stared at him numbly. Cam thought I was Pru. Or named Pru, anyway. I wasn't sure which was worse.

I tried to breathe, but my chest felt sore, as if all the air had been pushed out of me. This really was the most awful moment of my whole life. Almost getting arrested for grand theft auto didn't even come close.

I stared rigidly at Cam. "No," I said, "I am *not* Pru. I am terribly sorry to disappoint you."

The sore feeling in my chest got worse. Moving stiffly, I headed for the door. And then Cam grinned. "Gotcha!" he said, grabbing my arm. "Of course you're not Pru, you idiot. Pru didn't make that dynamite Dino-Rama. And she doesn't have that weird—but interesting—haircut," he added. "And like I said, I only have one extra ticket. So I flipped a coin, and it came up heads. You win."

"Great," I said. "This must be my lucky day."

Cam smiled. "Whew, that's a relief," he said. "For a minute there, I didn't think you had a sense of humor."

Mr. Gruenfeld walked up behind us. "A reporter has some questions for you," he told Cam.

"Be there in a second," Cam said. He looked at me. "Those movie passes are good for Friday," he said. "So . . . guess I'll see you at assembly, right?"

"Right," I said.

That was when I saw Nelson. He was standing behind Mr. Gruenfeld, watching me with an unreadable look on his face. I couldn't tell whether he'd heard Cam invite me to the movies or not. For a moment we just stood there, looking at each other.

Then he turned away and I hurried off to the girls' room, clutching my lipstick. But I couldn't help picturing Nelson sitting all by himself in the balcony at the Uptown Cinema, hunching his skinny shoulders as he plowed through a jumbo tub of buttered popcorn.

eighteen

~~~~~~~~~~~~~~~~~~~~~~~~~~~~~~~~

Compared with the way everything else turned out, the business with the room was a piece of cake.

When I got home, my father was in his study, lying on the sofa with a book over his face. I tapped on the open door.

"Uhhn," he said, which is his "Don't disturb me when I'm working on an article" noise, although it was a little muffled because of the book.

I sat down at his desk. "Working hard?" I asked.

My father grunted, and the book slid to the floor. "Thinking," he said. "Thinking is very hard work. History articles take a lot of planning." He sat up, looking rather grumpy.

"Guess what?" I said. "There was this art contest at school, and I did a project for it. And even though my project didn't win, you'll be pleased to know that I sold it."

"Good," my father said, still looking grumpy at having his article-planning interrupted. "I was starting to wonder how we were going to put both you kids through college. Keep up the good work."

He picked up his book. It was a mystery novel with a big yellow skull on the cover. I wondered what skulls had to do with planning history articles, but I decided not to ask.

Instead, I watched my father burrow back into the sofa. This was going to take more effort than I'd thought.

"A few months ago we had a conversation," I reminded him. "About this very study."

He paused in mid-burrow and glanced at me suspiciously. "Refresh my memory," he said.

I tried to keep my voice flat and neutral like a policeman presenting the facts. "Well," I said, "considering that you already have an office on campus and that your two nearly grown children are confined to horribly cramped quarters, I thought you might give me this study for my art work. I might even put my bed in here. For thinking purposes, naturally."

"Naturally," my father said.

I paused. Then I continued in my flat policeman voice, "At our last discussion, you stated that the day I sold a painting, I could have this study."

My father was glaring at me. I suddenly felt like Perry Mason addressing a hostile jury. I crossed my arms and took a deep breath. "Well, Dad, that day has come."

He fumbled to an upright position. "I demand to see an attorney! How do I know you sold anything? I want proof!"

"You can call Fred if you want," I said. Fred was my father's lawyer. "But you'd better tell him that I intend to sue for breach of contract if you go back on our deal." I wondered if you had to be eighteen to sue your own father. "And if you want proof, read tomorrow's paper. There's even a picture," I added. "You can show it to Fred when you tell him about the breach of contract."

"It was only a verbal agreement," my father said huffily. "It'll never hold up in court."

I sighed and stood up. "In that case," I said, "I guess I'll just have to tell Mom how you promised I could have your study. And I'm also going to have to tell her about the salami hidden in—"

My father sighed too. Slowly he got up off the couch. He looked around at his untidy bookshelves and his cluttered desk. "Never mind," he said defeatedly. "I guess it's time you had your own room, Mattie. I only hope you sell enough paintings to put yourself through law school. Though frankly, I don't think you'll need it."

"Thanks, Dad." I walked over and kissed him. "I really didn't want to have to sue you."

Then I stepped back and looked around the room. "Now," I said, "about the wallpaper."

"I have this great idea," Pru announced. "For a new club."

Heather glanced up from the stack of fashion magazines that littered the kitchen table. For the last half-hour we had been deciding which designer fashions we'd buy if we had a million dollars. So far Heather had chosen a $3,000 cocktail dress, and Pru was leaning toward the entire fall collection of Yves Saint Laurent. I'd decided to save my million and invest in real estate.

"We could design our own fashion magazine," Heather suggested. "For millionaires and their loved ones."

"How about a Paramedics Appreciation Society?" I said. "I know! We could invite our friends, and hide refreshments all over the house, and—"

"Come on," Pru said uncomfortably. "You've got to admit the Snickers bars have held up pretty well. A little squished, maybe, but still perfectly good. And I don't think you should make fun of the Paramedics," she added. "Arthur says they're going to make a video. They could be on MTV inside of a year."

It was Sunday again, and everything was back to normal. We were all getting pretty sick of hearing about Arthur, though. He was the drummer in Zee's band and the main reason Pru wasn't too upset when I beat her at gin rummy, or when I told her about Cam and the movie, or a few million other things. Pru had become a groupie.

Which was probably a good thing, because it explained why she wasn't at the assembly when Nelson and I got our honorable mention, and it almost explained the haircut. Almost.

As soon as the assembly was over, I'd rushed straight home to give Dad the good news. Afterward, I sat at my desk, making a list of the stuff I'd need now that Pru and I wouldn't be sharing a room anymore.

I paused to squint at the wallpaper. Maybe I'd go for something a little less flashy this time. I was getting pretty sick of that paisley, to tell the truth.

That was when Pru walked in and flopped triumphantly on the bed. "Well?" she said. "Do you like it?"

My notebook crashed to the floor. "Pru, you promised!—"

"I know I did, Mattie," Pru said, reaching up to touch her hair—her cute but unusual hair that looked like a cross between Zee Davis and a marine.

"It was Arthur," she explained. "He said he'd get me a great deal at this place where his cousin worked. He said all the Paramedics got their hair cut there." Pru giggled. "Arthur's cousin practically fainted when I walked in. He kept asking how my hair had grown out so fast."

I stared at her. "Ramon? You let *Ramon* cut your hair?"

Pru shrugged. "I don't remember his name, but I told him not to cut it too short."

Then she looked embarrassed. "I'm sorry, Mattie.

Honest. This Ramon guy must give everybody the same haircut."

"Come on, Pru," I said. "You missed the royal twin treatment. You couldn't face spending the rest of your life as a normie."

"That's not true!" Pru glared at me. "What was I supposed to do? Make the guy shave my head so that I wouldn't look like you?"

"It's a thought," I said hopefully.

"Besides," she added, "this stupid crew cut cost me forty dollars, which I personally don't think is much of a deal."

"Forty dollars? And you *paid* it?"

Pru eyed me warily. "Why? How much did yours cost?"

I looked at Pru's hair. Then I looked at the horses that covered half our room and at the paisley that covered the other half. Every once in a while, I figure, life offers you a trade-off. In this case, I got my own room and Pru got a stupid-looking haircut. All in all, it wasn't a bad exchange.

I picked up my notebook. "Look, considering I've survived more bad haircuts than you have, I'll let you in on a little secret. Don't make up your mind until you've stuck your head under the water faucet."

Pru looked mystified. "Does that mean you're not mad?" she said.

"And never pay more than twenty dollars for something you don't like."

"*Twenty?* But Arthur said—"

"Trust me," I said, and I headed down the hall to measure my new room for curtains. I wondered if Sur La Table carried draperies. I didn't think so, but you could never tell. Julia Child's kitchen just might have windows.

The next day I stood at the bulletin board, reading the *Post-Intelligencer* story about the Wyndham's contest. About the fifth time I read it, I got a sinking feeling in my stomach.

"Nelson Richfield and Mitzi Darwin, eighth graders at Seattle's Puget Sound Academy . . ."

Wonderful, I thought. The one time I had an actual moment of glory, I had to go down in history as "Mitzi."

But at least I'd gotten my name in the paper, sort of. And there was a big fuzzy picture of Nelson and me, staring stiffly at the camera and holding up our letter from the Science Center.

I stuck my head in the library, but there was no sign of Nelson. Maybe he was catching up on his postal chess. Or maybe the assembly had been too much for him. He might be lying on the plaid couch in the Richfields' living room, reading a book about inventors and eating mayonnaise on toast (my own favorite snack). Or maybe—

"There you are," said Heather. She sounded out of breath. "I've been looking all over for you."

"Well, I'm standing right here," I said. "Did you see this?" I pointed at the clipping. "It was on the very front page of the Living Section, and there's a picture of Nelson and me, except they got my name wrong."

Heather nodded. "That's why I was looking for you," she said. "I thought maybe we could do something tonight—you and me and Pru. To celebrate your becoming a celebrity. I thought maybe we could go to the movies," Heather said hopefully.

I stared at her. "Don't you have to practice, Heather? Or study?"

Heather smiled. It was a quiet, triumphant smile. "After the way I played at the Golden Goat opening, my dad finally realized that the world isn't losing a famous violinist, it's—"

"Losing a really terrible one?" I suggested.

Heather snorted. "I was *going* to say, gaining a famous costume designer. I showed him the sketches I did for the Paramedics, and Dad said maybe I could do the costumes for his barbershop quartet. They would require a very different look, of course."

"Of course," I said.

"So while I was at it, I told my mom that the best colleges want students who lead well-rounded lives. Lives that include going to the movies once in a while."

Heather paused. "Actually," she admitted, "it was *really* the sushi. Ever since that night at the Golden Goat, my mom and my aunt have been talking about opening a food stand down at the Public Market. It's taken her mind off me for a change."

"Well," I said, "I hope she'll give us her sushi recipe. It's the best-selling item on the Goat's menu."

Then I noticed a tall dark shape at the other end of the hall. For no reason my stomach suddenly decided to practice gymnastics. "Heather," I said, "I'm really glad you're not going to be playing the violin anymore. And I can't wait to see your costumes for the Paramedics. But I can't go with you tonight. I've . . . I've got a date. I'm going to see *Revenge of the Zombies* with Cam Davis."

"Really? With Cam?" Heather looked excited. Then her smile faded. "Are you sure that's a good idea, Mattie?"

"What do you mean, 'is it a good idea'? What kind of a question is that?"

Heather paused. "Nothing," she said. "But in case you hadn't noticed, Mattie, Nelson Richfield has a gigantic crush on you. Things could get messy. Love triangles are like that," she added. "There's one on *All of Our Days*, and —"

"Hang on a minute," I said. "Since when do you watch the soaps?"

She shrugged. "My mom tapes them. We started watching them together when we were making the sushi. Now I watch them all the time."

I groaned. "Oh, great. There goes Stanford."

The bell rang, and I smiled reassuringly at Heather. "Look, relax, okay? I know all about Nelson's crush, and it's nothing I can't handle."

She still looked worried. "Does Pru know?" she asked urgently. "About Cam?"

I sighed. "Good grief, Heather," I said. "I think you've been watching too much daytime drama." But as I left for class, it occurred to me that maybe Heather had a point.

I should have realized that night in the hedge. Nobody was named Cameron except on the soaps. And now it looked as if my life was turning into one.

By the time seven-thirty rolled around, I was getting pretty nervous. I was especially nervous about Pru. How did you tell someone who'd carved "Mrs. Cameron Davis" into the cover of her notebook that you were going to the movies with her future husband?

If you were me, you didn't say a word. If you were me, you hid in your room and spent a lot of time fooling around with your primrose lipstick and trying to figure out how to borrow Pru's pink sweater without telling her why you needed it.

It went something like this:

Me: I don't suppose you'd let me wear your pink sweater tonight.

Pru: Tonight? Why? Are you going somewhere?

Me: Uh, sort of . . .

Pru: What do you mean, "sort of"?

Me: Well, actually . . . I'm going to the movies. See, Cam felt sorry for Nelson and me because we didn't win first prize, and . . .

Pru: Oh, that. I already know about that. When Cam saw me at school today, he thought I was you. He ended up telling me the whole thing—all about his dad's free pass and flipping the coin and everything.

Me: He did? You do? So what about the sweater?

Pru: (shrugging) I guess you can wear it if you really want to. But don't get it all sweaty. I need it for band practice tomorrow.

Me: Band practice?

Pru: Arthur's teaching me to play the tambourine. And guess who we're getting for back-up vocals?

Me: I'm afraid to ask.

Pru: Lydia! We figure that way, if we get a gig in New York, the band can fly for free.

There was nothing to say. I told Pru she probably had a great future in show business and promised not to get her pink sweater too sweaty. Then I put it on and went downstairs to wait for Cam.

nineteen

Later that night, I sat in Dad's study and wrote in my journal. Things had gotten too hectic for poetry, which requires a certain amount of solitude and reflection. I'd decided to turn my book of poems into *The Collected Memoirs of Matilda Darwin*. By next summer I could probably fill an entire set of volumes.

"Volume I" (I wrote). "Here is all I can bring myself to report on my date with Cam. Cam wore a red-and-white rugby shirt and jeans. I wore Pru's pink sweater and sweated a lot, which Pru will not appreciate when she finds out. The movie was pretty scary in places, but not the kind where you have to watch it between your fingers."

I chewed on my pencil. This was the part I didn't want to write about. But what good was a journal if you didn't tell the truth?

"The next portion of the date is rather painful to report, to be perfectly honest. But here goes. During one of the non-scary parts, Cam got up to buy some

Raisinettes. I turned around to tell him to get me a Coke, and that is when I saw . . ."

I put down my pencil. Maybe I should have stuck to poetry. With poetry you could sort of hint at things that were too awful to talk about.

One of those things happened after I turned around in my seat at the Uptown Cinema. Because right behind me, sticking his hand into an enormous bin of popcorn, sat Nelson Richfield.

Just then, the zombies began blowing up someone's house. During the explosion my eyes met Nelson's. I hoped he would look away or maybe even leave, but he just sat there, gazing at me steadily.

"Nelson!" I snapped. "What are you doing here?"

"I'm watching a movie," he said calmly. "It isn't half-bad either. Want some?" He held out the tub of popcorn.

"No, I don't want any popcorn!" The people in the next seats turned and glared at me. "And I don't think you're here to watch some movie," I said, lowering my voice. "I think you're here to spy on me!"

Nelson shrugged. "It's a free country."

I turned back and tried to watch the movie, but it was impossible. I should have listened to Heather. What did I know about love triangles? I didn't watch daytime drama; that was another thing my mother disapproved of. Maybe if I had paid more attention to the soaps, I would know what to do, instead of sitting there turning Pru's sweater into a wet sponge.

After what seemed like a million years, during which the zombies demolished an entire town, Cam came back with his Raisinettes. I waited until he got the box open. Then I leaned over and reported, "Nelson is sitting right behind us."

Cam glanced back. He nodded at Nelson. Then he turned to me. "You're right," he said. "Want a Raisinette?"

I glared at my journal. After a moment, I picked up my pencil again.

"I always used to wonder why my mother rolled her eyes and said things like 'Men are impossible!' But now I'm beginning to understand. Because after the movie finished and the lights came up, Cam asked if I wanted to go get some pizza. And then . . ."

My handwriting was getting seriously messy. I gripped the pencil and hunched over the page. "And *then*, Cam turned to this person who had been sitting behind us, spying on me the whole time, and he asked this person if he would like to go have pizza too."

He had. He really had. Of course Nelson said yes. I remembered Nelson telling me about people who only loved one person their whole lives, and I tried to picture what the rest of my life would be like: Nelson showing up on every date I ever had. Nelson bursting into the church at my wedding, demanding that the ceremony be stopped. It wasn't exactly a rosy prospect.

So we went and had pizza, and I listened to Cam and

Nelson discuss model-building and basketball teams and hobbies. Cam was fascinated to learn about Nelson's postal chess, and Nelson seemed very interested to hear that Cam collected stamps. By the time we left the pizza parlor, they had decided to start a chess and stamp-collecting club at school, and Nelson promised he would see if they could use the library for meetings.

On the way home, Cam remarked that Pru and I were looking more identical these days.

"Don't remind me," I said. Or rather croaked, since my voice had pretty much dried up from non-use.

Cam smiled. "That'll make it tough if I want to invite you to the movies again," he said. "Maybe you should get a tattoo or something. So a person could tell you apart."

"Sure," I said. "How about a nice blue anchor right above my left elbow? That would be pretty distinctive, don't you think?"

By then we had reached the front steps. "Next time," Cam said, "maybe we should invite Nelson too. That way he won't have to stare at you over my shoulder for two hours."

"Or," I suggested, "we could just leave Nelson home."

Cam pretended to think it over. "You're right," he said after a moment. "But you know, I think your buddy Nelson is just lonely. I don't mean you're not worth staring at for two hours," he added. "But I bet once Nelson starts running that stamp club, he'll find other people to do things with." He smiled. "Things that hopefully won't include taking in *Bride from the Grave*. Next Friday? Eight sharp?"

I peered at Cam. Maybe, I thought, he wasn't impossible after all. Maybe he just understood men better than I did. Or Nelson Richfield, at any rate.

And maybe, I thought, as I closed my journal and crept down the hall to bed, I was pretty lucky to have someone like Cam Davis living right next door. Even if he did have blood-thirsty taste in movies.

"My new club," said Pru, "doesn't have anything to do with fashion magazines.

"Actually," she continued, as if it had just occurred to her, "I think that maybe it's time we let other people join. We could do stuff like take ferry rides or go up the Space Needle."

"Or visit famous natural food restaurants," Heather added. "We could call it the . . . the . . ."

But before Heather could call it anything, the doorbell rang. I put down the magazine article I'd been reading ("Short Cuts to Growing Out a Short Cut: Styles for that Awkward Stage") and went to answer it.

Nelson stood at the front door. When he saw me, he gave a nervous twitch.

"Hi," he said. "I came to apologize for spying on you the other night."

"That's okay, Nelson," I said. "It happens all the time."

Nelson paused in mid-twitch. "It does?"

I leaned against the door. "Sure. Why, just the other day on *All of Our Days,* Brad followed Cheryl to her lunch appointment with Rod, and he hid in the next booth and . . ."

Nelson stared at me. "Mattie," he said. "Do you feel all right?"

"It's this love triangle on daytime television," I told him. "The point is, you don't have to feel like a jerk, Nelson. Just don't do it again."

"I won't," he said. Then he paused and squinted at me. "So do you think Cam falls into the third twin category, by any chance?"

"Definitely not," I said. "Cam falls into the friend category. And just because I've got other friends, that doesn't mean I'm not your friend, Nelson. It doesn't work that way."

Nelson sighed. "I know. But it takes awhile to figure this stuff out."

"I'm sure you'll get the hang of it," I told him, but Nelson squinted at me skeptically.

Then I thought of something. "Nelson, remember that day at the Science Center, when you told me evolution doesn't happen overnight? You were talking about me and Pru. But you might try a little evolving yourself."

I took a deep breath. "Join the human race, Nelson. Let's face it, the haircut was a start, but you still have a long way to go."

"What do you mean?" Nelson muttered. "I happen

to consider myself fully evolved, if it's all the same to you."

I sighed. "Let's talk fashion here, Richfield. You could start by spending some of that Dino-Rama money at Wyndham's. Maybe some chess fiend in Wichita doesn't care if you wear horrible plaid sport shirts or goofy-looking shoes. But I do, Nelson."

He looked pained. "You do?"

"I like you in spite of it, so stop looking so wounded. All I'm saying, Nelson, is that I'm finally learning there's more to life than being a twin. So maybe you could learn there's more to life than aquariums and microscopes. Or sitting alone at the movies, for that matter. The point is, a little adaptation wouldn't kill you either. After all," I added, "look what happened to the dinosaurs. You don't want to end up in a glass case somewhere. 'Nelsonus Richosaurus. Thirteen-year-old misfit inventor. Now extinct.' Just ask Uncle Charlie about *that*."

Nelson smiled sourly. "I don't think Charles Darwin had *Revenge of the Zombies* in mind when he came up with the theory of evolution."

"Charles Darwin might have loved *Revenge of the Zombies*! He might have found zombies completely fascinating."

Nelson still looked skeptical, but he seemed a little less twitchy. I paused and peered at him. Then I said, "Nelson, would you like to come in? You could stay for dinner if you want. Unless my mother's trying out a new recipe, in which case you might want to skip it."

Nelson nodded. "I—" he started to say.

Then he stopped and turned, and we both stared.

Someone was making his way through the hedge. Someone, in fact, a lot like Cam Davis. In another moment he'd be heading straight for the front steps, looking, as usual, like he'd just stepped out of the pages of a teen fashion magazine.

So much for pep talks. I watched Cam stride across the lawn. Then I looked at Nelson, who was busy glaring at Cam, and I wished that my life would stop resembling a soap opera for about thirty seconds.

Sometimes weird things happen when you make a wish.

"Mattie?" a voice called. "What are you . . .?"

It was my mother. She was wearing a very stained Sur La Table apron, and her hair was falling out of her braid in damp red tendrils.

"I was just about to ask if Heather wanted to stay for pizza," she said. "I've been wrestling with this osso bucco all afternoon, and I'm too tired to cook anymore."

"What's osso bucco?" I asked, just as Cam reached the front porch.

"Ox knuckles," Nelson said. He glanced at me and shrugged. "I've only read about it, but it's supposed to be very good. But pizza sounds fine too."

"Hey, pizza!" Cam said. He clapped Nelson heartily on the back. "Is my timing good or what? Must have been ESP: Especially Starving for Pizza."

I gave him a baleful look.

But Sally smiled. "That settles it, then," she said. "We can order an extra-large. I hope you don't mind anchovies," she added. Cam and Nelson shook their heads.

She held the door open, and we watched them troop off toward the kitchen. Then I turned and stared at Sally. "*Pizza*, Mom? You'd really order a big oily pizza, loaded with lethal sodium and nitrates and . . ."

My mother wiped her face with a corner of her apron. "Hey, give me a little credit for fast thinking here. Believe it or not, Mattie, I really was thirteen years old once. Although I can't say I ever had two boys show up at the same time."

"It's okay, Mom." I turned and glanced back at the kitchen. "Just this once, I think we have enough Darwins to go around. But you might want to order another pizza," I added. "I mean, we're dealing with *boys* here, Mom."

My mother looked at me and laughed. "You're right," she said. "It's been a long time since I was thirteen."

"Here is what happened after the pizzas arrived" (I wrote that night). "Nelson told Pru about his twin tastebud theory. She thought it was very interesting, but she wasn't sure she wanted to be my official taster if I ever became a foreign dictator. Then Heather took me aside and said I seemed to be handling the triangle situation very maturely. I told her that in my opinion Nelson just needed to be more involved in things. She looked very impressed and immediately went off to invite him to join Pru's new club. Nelson agreed, on the condition that it didn't involve driving without a license.

"At that point Dad came home, and pretty soon he and Cam and Nelson were in the living room discussing World War II sea battles. (This seems to be a serious affliction of the male species, but if my mother can get used to it, I guess I can too.)

"Right before he left, Cam mentioned something about a tennis clinic at the health club, and would I be interested in attending. I said that yes, I would be.

"Then Arthur came to get Pru for band practice. My parents left to take the osso bucco over to the Golden Goat and to give Nelson a ride home.

"Heather had to go see *Madame Butterfly*, so she went home to change. That left me alone to finish off what was left of the second pizza. Except there wasn't any, because Winston had jumped in the box when no one was looking and demolished every last anchovy."

At that point, the door opened and Pru walked in. She looked around the room. My father's desk and books were still there, plus five rolls of Spring Bouquet wallpaper, but we had managed to squeeze my bed in next to them, along with a new dresser from Sears.

"Hi," she said. "I saw the light on."

"Hi." I closed my journal. "How was Paramedics practice?"

"Fine." She sat down on the bed. "Actually, I've been home for a while. I've been rearranging our room," she added. "It feels pretty weird having the whole place to myself."

"I know what you mean," I said. "But you'll probably like it after a while."

"Yeah, probably." Pru paused. "What I mean is, I miss . . ." She stopped and chewed thoughtfully on a fingernail. "I miss the way we used to talk," she said. She sounded embarrassed. "You know, after we turned the lights out and stuff. And now . . ."

I sighed. "I know. I couldn't fall asleep either."

There were definitely bad sides to being a twin. Somehow I'd forgotten about the good ones. Like how great it was to have someone to talk to at night, especially someone with the same temperament, and the same tastebuds, and the same sense of humor. Maybe Mom was right and I'd marry a person like that someday. But by then I'd probably be a total insomniac.

I looked at my five rolls of Spring Bouquet wallpaper. Then I looked at Pru. She was scrunched up at the foot of the bed, gnawing on her fingernails and staring at me miserably.

Finally I grabbed a pillow and threw it down to Pru.

"This will still be my room," I told her as she settled under the covers. "And that will still be your room. But a brief period of adjustment probably isn't a bad idea."

"Just until we get used to the new arrangement," Pru agreed.

After a moment, I crawled under the blanket and reached up to turn out the light. "Good-night, Prune," I said into the darkness.

There was a brief pause.

Then I heard a muffled noise from the foot of the bed. It sounded like a snicker.

"Good-night, *Mitzi,*" Pru said.

About the Author

Mary E. Ryan was born in Manchester, New Hampshire, two minutes after her identical twin sister, Margaret. She and her sister grew up together in Tempe, Arizona, but attended different colleges and have pursued separate career paths.

Mary E. Ryan is the author of two young adult novels, *Dance a Step Closer* and *I'd Rather Be Dancing*, and her short fiction has appeared in many magazines. She holds a degree in filmmaking from New York University and the master's degree in writing from the University of Washington in Seattle, where she lives.

Although her sister, who has degrees in communications and journalism, lives in Palm Beach, Florida, the twins stay in touch, not necessarily through ESP.